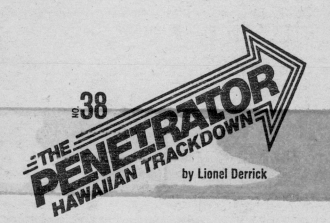

THE PENETRATOR

NO. 38

HAWAIIAN TRACKDOWN

by Lionel Derrick

PINNACLE BOOKS   LOS ANGELES

THE PENETRATOR #38:
HAWAIIAN TRACKDOWN

An original Pinnacle Books edition, published for the first time anywhere.

First printing, October 1980

ISBN: 0-523-40923-0

Special acknowledgement to Chet Cunningham

Cover illustration by George Wilson

Printed in the United States of America

PINNACLE BOOKS, INC.
2029 Century Park East
Los Angeles, California 90067

DEADLY DECISION

Mark hurried toward the end of the hallway, where he saw brighter lights and could hear excited voices. A panel opened just in front of him, and an unsuspecting black man came into the hall. He saw Mark and lifted his hands silently. Mark's burp gun centered on his chest.

"Turn around slow, friend, or eat lead." The man turned slowly, anger and frustration on his face. Mark slammed the receiver of the weapon across the fuzzy black head, and the man crumpled. The Penetrator jumped over the man and ran lightly to the end of the hallway.

A two-story section opened in front of him. Thirty feet across the room, Mark saw Preacher Mann towering over five or six excited women bunched in front of him. Everyone seemed to be shouting.

"Preacher Mann. Don't move. I've got a machine gun trained on your big gut. Move and I'll plaster you all over the tatami!"

Preacher Mann's big arm swung out and trapped two women in front of him and pulled them closer to his own bulk.

"Go ahead, Penetrator. If you're good enough to miss them and hit me, blast away. These are innocent people here." Preacher Mann laughed as Mark hesitated; then he dragged the girls backward, jumped into an elevator, and closed the door.

Six others in the room began firing at Mark. He sent several rounds at them and charged for a curved stairway to his left. He was out of sight of the shooters in a few seconds, moving upward cautiously. He had no idea of the terrain, and he knew that the Preacher had all the cards, all the troops. . . .

THE PENETRATOR SERIES:

CONTENTS

HAWAIIAN TRACKDOWN

PROLOGUE

Mark Hardin is the Penetrator, a man absolutely devoted to stamping out crime, corruption, and assaults on the elderly, the poor, those who can't defend themselves from the common enemy.

He knew it would not be easy. Whenever one man challenges the entire criminal element of society, he understands that the odds are stacked against him. Mark was used to such odds, and that meant having the nation's law enforcement agencies as well as countless underworld hit men after him. To most police details, the Penetrator was as bad as any criminal, because he usually operated outside the law, functioned as a super-vigilante with immediate justice at the end of a deadly .45 round.

At times Mark wondered if he were losing the battle. For him the essence called life was a walk along a desperate straightedge between the legal and criminal, between good and evil; and hundreds kept trying to force him off into one side or the other.

He knew all this when he began. Still he dove in.

As the Penetrator, he had been battling crime for longer than he wants to remember. It all began when hoodlums killed his fiancée and tried to kill him at the same time in a fiery auto crash in California. That triggered his one-man assault on crime, and he has been at it ever since. He used the money he liberated from criminals for his own operating bankroll, and the treasury was never empty.

He had a base of operations in California, but it was one he seldom saw for long anymore. Help came from Professor Willard Haskins and an ancient Indian, David Red Eagle, both at the professor's secret hideaway, camouflaged in an old borax mine near Barstow in the desert.

But Mark worked alone in the field. His assistants were only office and backup help at the Stronghold. Out on a mission he was on his own.

The Penetrator's natural ability as a warrior came from his Indian heritage. In the Vietnam war he had taken that native talent and sharpened and honed his fighting skills to a fine and deadly edge, mastering every handheld fighting tool the army could supply him. He became a weapons expert. David Red Eagle had dug into Mark's background and proved that he was half Cheyenne, and then had trained him in the quiet, careful, effective, and the deadly best of Indian fighting techniques.

In his years of battles, the Penetrator's body had picked up dozens of scars, more than a bullfighter or professional football player. He had been shot, stabbed, slashed, and had broken more bones than he could remember. He knew he was living at the end of a short fuse, on shattering ice. He couldn't be lucky forever. One of these days he would be a fraction of an inch too far one way, or move a millisecond too late, and his last mission would be over.

Until that time came, the Penetrator was a one-man

terror for the crime world, from the huge syndicates to the small-town hoods. Everywhere the corrupters had heard of him and feared him. They knew he could not be bought, that he used tactics as basic, effective, and illegal as they did, and that he was a thousand percent dedicated to ending their crime careers and perhaps their lives as well if that's what it took.

It made the Penetrator a deadly enemy. He was interested in only one thing for himself—his life. For Mark Hardin, life was the ultimate factor. Without survival his work was over; therefore he tried to survive—not at any cost, but if at all possible, because survival meant the continuation of his work, and it wasn't finished.

The Penetrator had been led all over the world on his exploits. Wherever he traced terrorism or crime and corruption he fought it, from Japan to France, from Mexico to the Caribbean, from the depths beneath the sea to the soaring reaches of outer space in a manned satellite.

The Penetrator was not a part-time player, not a specialty team man. He went both ways on offense and defense: he played the game with his life and every dollar in the world he owned or could steal from the Mafia and organized crime, and he came out a winner.

Now, on one of those rare times, he was relaxing in the Stronghold, looking over the status board, trying to select a new target. There were so many. The Professor kept a board filled with the names of current hot spots numbered from one to ten. Each numbered slot had a file folder with a description of the situation, recent press clippings, and reports from the police teletype that chattered away in the communications room.

The police wire was there due to some minor connivance with a longtime friend on the Los Angeles sheriff's department, and with it the Penetrator could know what was going on in many different parts of the nation which local newspapers and network broadcasts didn't think were important.

He had been back at the Stronghold for almost three days now, and he was getting nervous. Inactivity sometimes did that to him. Mark took a fifteen-mile jog in the desert, and when he came back he showered, shaved, and tried to relax.

But he couldn't. He paced the floor of the communications room, looking again and again at the status board. Ten projects all demanding attention, each as important as any other. Which one should he choose?

CHAPTER 1

Supply and Demand

J. Ashton Monroe sat in his real estate office in La Jolla, California, and glanced at the afternoon newspaper. It was after 8:00 in the evening and he was the only one left in the office. He was waiting for a man who had phoned earlier, a "live" one who seemed genuinely interested in a twenty-four unit apartment. He had learned to tell the serious buyers from the lookers. The man said he would be in about 8:00, that his name was Culbertson, and he needed to make a purchase quickly for tax purposes.

The pleasant idea of a commission on the $800,000 apartment complex was quashed when Monroe looked back at the newspaper. He read the San Diego *Union* headline, hardly able to believe it: "TWO JAILED IN CHILD PORNO RING"

Then he read the story below the bannerline:

"Anthony Cuzo and Harold J. Billingham were arrested today on charges of violating the California child sex abuse laws, according to a report from the San

Diego district attorney's office. Both men were charged with sexual misconduct with children, contributing to the delinquency of a minor, oral sex with a minor, and various other unnatural sex acts with children.

"Both men pleaded innocent and were released on $50,000 bond each. Both Cuzo and Billingham are local businessmen, and neither has had previous criminal records. Neighbors of both expressed shock and total surprise at the indictments and arrests.

"Informants on the street who know the San Diego scene say little is known about this phase of the sexual activity in the city. Such pedophilic activities are usually shrouded in secrecy, even within a family, and experts say incest is often the starting point of such activities. Vice officers here indicated the local operation included a large amount of professional photography and that the pictures were being used in a commercial operation.

"Vice squad members say they have known for some time of commercial pedophilic activities here, but this is their first break. They indicated information came on a tip from an informer, and more arrests would be made in the future."

J. Ashton threw the paper into the wastebasket. Suddenly he was sweating. He felt the beads of perspiration break out on his forehead and reached in a desk drawer for some tissue. Then he read more of the article. The police had raided a private home and confiscated cameras, prints, negatives, and other equipment. The police surprised the men involved in photography of children and adults in nude and compromising situations and positions. The two children involved were minors and were released to their parents.

Monroe wiped his forehead. He was a large man, well over six-foot-three and weighed two hundred and

6

forty pounds. His face was firm, clean-shaven, skin-tight. He prided himself that, at thirty-two, he had kept himself in perfect condition. His vested suit was neatly in fashion, and his thick brown hair cut moderately between the business trim of ten years ago and the current ear-hiding style.

He wiped his forehead again, and felt wetness under his arms. Why did he always sweat when he was nervous? An immediate surge in his heart rate and blood pressure too, he imagined.

God! He never thought it would come to this. Not publicity, not right in the newspaper! And he didn't even know those two men, Cuzo and Billingham. How in hell had he got mixed up in all this in the first place. He thought back and scowled. It had been so simple, and so innocent.

He was involved with a girl, Susie, a pretty little thing with a good body who didn't mind sharing now and then. One night she told him she was into nudism and was a member of a sunshine club. She asked him to come to a weekend in the country out at the "farm."

Hell, nudism wasn't anything; they even had a legal nude beach within five miles of his office down past La Jolla Shores. No big thing. She persuaded him to go. It was summer then and they all stripped and played volleyball and went swimming in the pool. It was a blast, and he had never seen so many boobies bouncing around in his life. Absolutely nothing sexy happened.

The next week Susie told him about this chance they had to get some pictures from their club in the *Sunshine & Health* magazine, a national publication devoted to nudism. They wanted him to pose with some of them. He said absolutely not. A week later, in her bedroom, Susie persuaded him to do it.

It started out innocently enough. Three couples.

They posed in a little makeshift studio set up in a garage at a private home. They shot two rolls of film and then somebody popped some beers and some mixed drinks and before he knew it they were posing again, and things were a little hazy for him. He did realize the thing was getting out of hand. Everyone seemed sexed up, and one couple was making it on a couch in the corner. He had another drink and then they brought in the two kids, both naked too, and about ten years old, a little boy and a little girl.

The kids had drinks too and got involved in the posing and picture-taking and Monroe found that he was the center of attention with the kids and cameras. It was so fuzzy he soon didn't really know what was happening. He did remember that Susie had driven him home and helped him into his room. He was bombed.

The next day he had a hangover he couldn't shake and he called Susie and broke it off between them. He remembered just enough to make him not want to have anything more to do with that crowd.

Then he got the picture in the mail. He was in it and so were both the kids. He couldn't believe it. The rest of the day J. Ashton Monroe was physically ill. He couldn't go to work.

Two days later he got the first call. He hung up. By the time he had received the call from the same man six times, he listened. If he didn't cooperate they would ruin him in La Jolla. They would send the police the pictures, get him thrown in jail, and have him labeled as an MDSO, a Mentally Disordered Sex Offender. That tag would follow him the rest of his life. They also would have one of the parents of the little girl press charges, and put him away in jail for at least twenty years. He must know that child molesters usually lasted only six to seven months in prison before the other inmates killed them.

J. Ashton Monroe caved in. After that he did what they told him—went where they told him and let them take their filthy pictures. He was terrified, but they had him hooked so tightly he knew he could never get away. Sometimes they let him wear masks and hide his face, but what they made him do with the children was disgusting, degrading.

Then one day a plainclothes vice-squad man talked to him. The police had identified him in a picture someone had sent them. They didn't know how deeply he was involved. But if he didn't cooperate with them, they would charge him, throw him in jail, tag him with the MDSO label. So he had threats from both sides. But the police offered him complete immunity and protection if he gave them names, dates, photo setups, everything he could remember.

They in turn would raid the studios, the labs, get every negative, every print, and protect him. These people who were using him were not hardened criminals, not Mafia goons, the police assured him. They might threaten him and make lots of phone calls, but that would probably be all. So he gave them everything they asked for, two weeks ago. And now the first arrests.

Now that he had thought about it again, he was afraid. He had no idea how much money was involved, how many prints they sold, even what they did with them. He had seen some in magazines aimed at sick people who were real pedophiles. He still might have to move to another town; he might be ruined here despite what the police told him. He had seen an SD police car outside the office for a while that afternoon, but it was gone now.

9

He glanced up at the front door of the real estate firm on Prospect Street. The door was unlocked, he was waiting to meet Mr. Culbertson, who was ten minutes late now. Hell, he probably wasn't coming. It was amazing the high percentage of people who said they would come and never did. No-shows in real estate calls must be nearly fifty percent. Culbertson was just another one. If he called tomorrow they could set it up again. Damn, even one and a half percent of $800,000 was a lot of cash.

Someone opened the front door, and Monroe glanced up in a moment of panic. The man walked in and held out his hand.

"Sorry I'm late. I'm Culbertson and I'm inquiring about that twenty-four unit apartment."

"Yes, yes, I'm Monroe. Sit down right here, Mr. Culbertson. I have all the details in my file." He looked down at the file and then glanced back at the man called Culbertson. Yes, he was all right: he was well dressed, about forty, pleasant manner. No threat or worry there. Monroe reached into his lower file drawer and took out another set of papers he thought he might use. He liked to have all the items handy that had any bearing on a deal.

When he looked back at the customer he saw only the black barrel of a pistol with a long black silencer on it.

"What in the world?"

"I think you know, Mr. Monroe."

"But I don't!"

"You should ask Mr. Cuzo and Mr. Billingham. I'm sure they would want to have a long talk with you, but this way is better. Good-bye, Mr. Monroe."

The weapon fired with a soft clucking sound and the .45 caliber bullet went through Monroe's forehead, smashing into his brain, churning, tearing, and mashing vital brain centers into a froth of blood, lifeless tissue, and bone.

Monroe slumped backward in his chair, eyes vacant, staring at the wall. The gunman moved closer and fired seven more rounds from the .45 automatic, sending them all into Monroe's crotch; then he turned and walked out the front door. As near as the gunman could tell, no one had noticed him come or leave.

Two salesmen and a secretary arriving at the real estate office the next morning found J. Ashton Monroe.

The tall black man smiled. "Look, Mama, we always pay good, don't we? You get your cash right on the countertop. Nobody hassling you. The cops don't know you're alive no more. Come on, Mama, you getting a twinge of conscience, now?"

The slender black woman shrugged and slipped on her bra, fitted it over large breasts, and fastened it in front. "Buck, honey. You are a great stud, and you pay your bills and don't get me in no trouble. You just standing there looking at me gets me so horny I want to lay back down and go again. But the picture shit, I just can't do it no more. I mean those little kids. What do they know? Sure I can take the pictures, and most of the kids don't give a damn, but I do."

She stepped into soft blue nylon panties, pulled on a wraparound skirt, and a blue blouse.

"So I'm telling you out front. You got the last pictures from me you're going to get. I just can't do this shit no more."

The smile was gone from Buck's face. He came away from the door, his brown suit sleekly expensive over an open-collared tan silk sport shirt.

"Mama, you saying you trying to quit on me?" The

11

voice was hard, the inflection disbelieving. "Look, you the best supplier I got. The big man says I send him the best black meat he's seen, and he likes the salt and pepper jazz you throw in. No way I can let you quit."

The girl shook her hair; it was set in a million tiny ringlets. "Buck, honey, you don't understand. I didn't make up my mind like some dumb black bitch. I thought this out slow and easy, for two months. The bread, I need the bread, but I can always go back to the street. At least out there I'm the one taking the shit and not the kids. You ever think what these young kids gonna think of us when they grow up? What they gonna think of me?" She turned and went to the window of the small room and stared down at Amsterdam Avenue in Harlem. "No way, Buck. Just no way I'm gonna take any more goddamn dirty pictures of kids for you!"

When she turned to look back at him, she gasped. The wide, heavy blade went in just over her navel, plunged six inches into her soft belly and then sliced upward, twisting and tearing as it came out, leaving a wasteland of ruptured and sliced-in-half vital tubes, arteries, and intestines. She sagged against the knife, then slid to the floor. Buck bent and wiped the blade on her skirt, then looked down at her and the blood splattering his suit.

"Mama, I'm sorry. You was a good woman, best I've ever had. But this had to be. Nobody quits the Mann, you knew that. I told you way back. We can't leave loose strings, and Mama, you just came a big long loose one. It was great for a while."

She stared at him from the floor, both hands held to her intestines, and tried to stop the flow of blood. Her eyes fluttered, then opened, and she writhed and thrashed.

"Maybe it's the best way," she moaned. "Leastways,

you bastard, I won't have to look at those big brown eyes staring up at me and asking my why without even asking. God that hurts! You cut me bad, Buck. Finish it!"

"Won't take long, Mama, and I got to be out and away from here by then." He went to the closet, took out a suitcase, and checked the contents. "This all your negatives, the whole file?"

"Yeah, you son of a bitch. I tried to burn them a dozen times, you know that? I honest to God tried."

"Sorry, Mama." He went out the door and let it lock behind him.

She lay on the floor, bleeding to death inside and out. The lights seemed to fade. She watched the window, and then tried to look down at her stomach. She couldn't see it.

She was right. It was good to be out of it. She hadn't accomplished much in her twenty-eight years, and the last two had been the worst. But at least she didn't have to do it anymore. Yeah, it was best this way. She told Buck she quit, and she had. Never again would she take any more pictures for them. Never more. Her eyes closed and her head turned slowly to the left before the one long last breath gushed from her stilled lungs.

The small bookshop was well off the Loop, but everyone who wanted to know about it did, and knew how to find it. The front was a bookstore and newsstand, with the best-sellers and about 3,000 other paperback titles, magazines, and hometown newspapers. In back of that came the normal mix of "adult" pornographic books, with covers showing suggestive poses and some downright graphic ones. In back of them were the racks for the sex films they don't show in school and two big cases of sexual devices to get your partner sexed up in a rush.

Behind these counters was a plain oak desk with nothing on the top. If you didn't know what was sold at the desk, you didn't belong there. No one answered any questions.

A woman in her mid-thirties with two women's magazines under her arm stood at the desk waiting. A peephole in the wall opposite the desk showed one brown eye for a second; then the door opened and a clerk ambled up to the desk. The woman handed him a piece of paper and he vanished into the back of the store. A few minutes later he came out with a paper sack carefully stapled at the top. He took $45 from the woman and nodded. She put a brown envelope on top of *Good Housekeeping* magazine and walked out of the shop through the front door.

Lester lifted his eyes, pushed a finger under his nose, and pushed back his head. "Goddamn snooty broads," he mumbled as he went through the door again into the back room. The back of the store was small, about twenty feet each way, and stacked with boxes of books and magazines. All the material back here was in their porno line. The legitimate books and magazines were all serviced by the wholesaler on a consignment basis, by the wholesale distributor, Illinois Periodicals, Inc.

The porno books were direct from the publishers, some on consignment, others direct purchases. And there were magazines too, like the woman had just bought. Lester had no idea how guys or women got their kicks looking at naked pictures of kids who weren't even sexually developed. He closed the box from which he had just filled the order. The title of the magazine was *Life Child*. On the cover a black naked girl of about twelve sat looking at a naked white boy of ten.

14

Lester shook his head, closed the top of the box, and went back to unpacking books.

A bell rang three times and he went to the alley door, looked through a peephole, and grinned. Lester opened the two locks, and swung the door wide.

"Hi there, Charlie, you son of a bitch. How's it going?"

"In and out, up and down, man. You found a new way?"

They both laughed. Charlie was in his twenties, black, and dressed sharply with at least four hundred dollars' worth of casual clothes.

"Got a shipment for you, man," Charlie said.

"Christ, Charlie, you was just by here three days ago. I don't think we need any more of your slicks."

Charlie lost his grin. "Don't say that, Lester. We've got some extras, we had to close down one guy. There's gonna be lots more buyers around here. Go get Adolph, he'll have to decide."

Lester shrugged and walked to the small offices at the front of the store with its one-way mirror and told the owner, Adolph Jurgen, the problem.

Jurgen was a small round man, five-feet four-inches tall, about forty-five years old, and a hundred and eighty pounds. He rolled bloodshot eyes to the ceiling.

"That creep pushing more of his asshole skin books? We've got too many from the last time."

"These are the fifteen dollar magazines, Adolph. The kiddy porn things."

"I know what the hell they are. I'll get rid of the slob." Adolph opened his desk drawer, took out a .38 with a four-inch barrel, and pushed it in the front of his belt so it was obvious. Then he walked to the shipping room.

Charlie got in the first round.

"Morning, Adolph, good to see you again. I got that next shipment I told you about, twenty-five copies of each of our three books. Knew you were running short. Bring your checkbook?"

Adolph stared at him, then shook his head. "I'm going broke, you black bastard, and I'm not buying any more of your skin books until I sell the ones I have. You overloaded me last week; don't you remember that? And you don't take them back—no consignment. So to hell with you, Charlie. Now get your ass out of my store."

"Hey, hey, that's not friendly at all, Adolph. You got a quota, man. That was the arrangement. You sell them or you don't, not none of my worry. But you take your quota!"

"No fucking hardnose is coming into my store and tell me . . ." Adolph was so mad he could hardly control his hands. He stabbed for the revolver and Charlie threw a round kick that caught Adolph's hand just as it touched the weapon, slamming his hand away from the .38 and skittering the gun across the floor.

Charlie took advantage of his training in full contact karate and did a spinning backkick. His right foot swung five feet high, and the heel of his heavy platform shoe arched down and hit Adolph on the side of the neck just under his ear. Adolph groaned and slumped to the floor.

"Jesus, Jesus, Jesus . . ." Lester mumbled. "Christ, you've killed him, Charlie!"

"Naw, just a little spin-back kick. He'll be all right. These heavier shoes do put more sting in it though. Look at that. I knocked out the little shit! I never did that in twenty fights in the full-contact karate ring! Well, fun time's over." He fished in Adolph's pocket and came up with his fat wallet.

16

Charlie pulled bills off the roll and put them in a stack.

"Count it, Lester. There should be nine-hundred and thirty-eight dollars there. That's seventy-five copies at twelve-fifty each. You tell Adolph I took only what he owed me, and I'll be back in two weeks, unless he wants extra copies. And you start pushing our books, man. Hell, Adolph could go broke if he lets them stack up. Give them some shelf space." He straightened, wrote out a receipt, and dropped it on Adolph's chest.

"There you go, man. Let me know if you need any more of the kiddie books. I got plenty, and that's all I sell, so remember me."

Charlie peeled a twenty dollar bill off his roll and tossed it to Lester. "Here, man, no hard feelings. Nothing personal, you know that, just business. You understand, don't you, Lester?"

"Yeah, sure, just business." Lester picked up the twenty and stuffed it in his pocket. Then he went to the alley and unloaded the three stacks of magazines from a big blue Cadillac and carried the skin books into the shop. After he locked the rear door he looked down at his boss.

Lester got a wet cloth and put it on Adolph's forehead. He wasn't sure if Adolph was alive or dead, and he didn't know how to check.

As the cold cloth touched Adolph's temples, he groaned, his eyes popped open, and he sat up swearing and reaching for the .38 that wasn't there.

"Goddamnit!" Adolph said and stared at the closed back door.

CHAPTER 2

Anybody's Grandmother

Deep in the communications room of the Stronghold near Barstow, California, Mark Hardin watched the police wire for a while, found nothing interesting, and went back to the status board. He slid over the first two categories and stopped at the one marked number three.

"PEDOPHILIA" the card read. He wasn't sure exactly what the word meant, but he knew it had something to do with sexual perversion. He took out the file and began, reading first the story from the San Diego *Union*, then one from New York telling about the death of a young black woman.

"B. J. Parks evidently knew she was in a dangerous situation, because, in her private effects, investigators found a safe deposit box key. Vice-squad officers refused to say what they found when they got a court order to open the box, but they all were smiling. It was rumored to be a gold mine of names, addresses, and contacts in the New York pedophilia scene, and they predicted that the sexual mistreatment of children in that area should be remarkably reduced due to the find.

"There was nothing substantial in the box or in the apartment to help lead to the discovery of who the killer might be, police reported. A knife was used, and detectives are now checking out several close friends of B. J. Parks who might know more about the death than they are admitting.

"Police say they also will be searching for any casual or close friends of Miss Parks who have no visible means of support, and may have been involved in the pedophilic ring that was supplying large numbers of pictures of children in sex situations.

"It was the first time that police indicated the sex-picture business was involved. B. J. Parks was well known in some areas as a photographer."

Mark went on to other stories in various cities that told of similar activities. It looked as if there was some kind of an organized effort in the country to produce photo sets and printed magazines that promoted pedophilia.

The Penetrator grew more restive and aggravated as he read. The very idea of using children in such a filthy racket both shocked and angered him.

The last clipping was from the Los Angeles *Times* three days ago. One John Califona had just been convicted on twelve counts of sexual perversion, including the forcing of his daughter to participate in unnatural sexual acts for a photographer. The father was part of a group selling such photos to an unnamed printer. The case broke when the daughter, who was thirteen, but could pass for eleven, confided to her minister what was going on. The minister took the girl directly to the juvenile division of the office of the Los Angeles sheriff, who began the investigation, and brought charges.

John Califona and a partner in the scheme were convicted and sentenced to from seven to fifteen years in prison. The next day Califona's daughter, Melinda, was killed by four shots fired from a passing car as she walked to school.

Mark took the file and marched in to where Professor Willard Haskins sat reading in the Stronghold. Mark dropped the file on the Professor's book and glared at it.

"Professor, just how long has this sort of thing been going on?"

Professor Haskins smiled. "Probably for fifteen to twenty thousand years from what archaeologists tell us. Certainly such problems were known to the Phoenicians and in ancient Egypt, and the Roman Empire rather prided itself on the diversity of its sexual aberrations. But I know that wasn't what you asked, Mark. This current upsurge of activity does seem rather unusual. It may be chance. Or it may be that the practice is being promoted and in such promotion some people were used who either turned informer or, by some clever method, left evidence for the authorities. I'd lean toward the latter explanation."

"And you think it's widespread in this country?"

"With the sexual mores relaxing I'd say yes, perhaps with the exception of the southern Baptist states."

"They're just kids; they are the innocent victims. What are they going to think, how are they going to react, when they grow up? How can they be anywhere near emotionally stable? The psychological problems are so far-reaching."

"Yes, Mark, but since neither you nor I are psychologists, can you think of anything else we might do about the problem?"

"Cut off the head of the printing empire, and there

20

would be no need for, and no market for, the large number of pictures."

"True. But then you need to find the head of the creature. How can you do that?"

"Professor, I'm not sure, but I think it's time I had a long talk with my old cop friend with the Los Angeles sheriff's office."

"Oh, yes, Captain Patterson. Give him my regards."

"I'll do that, Professor." Mark left the room, went back to the communications center, and consulted a card file. He found the name: Patterson, Captain Kelly, and dialed the Los Angeles bypass number they used so nothing could be traced to the Stronghold. He finished dialing and waited for the five-second buzz; then he heard a new dial tone. Now that he was on an untraceable Los Angeles line, Mark dialed the last number he had for Kelly and waited. It took him four calls to track him down. Kelly's current assignment was captain in charge of the day watch at one of the north county divisions.

"Captain Kelly Patterson himself?" Mark asked.

"Yes, who's this?"

"This, Kelly, is your Indian friend who doesn't like to climb cliffs any more than you do."

"Well, son of an eagle's feather, what the hell you doing? Are you in town, around the corner, how about dinner?"

"I'm still in the hole, Kelly, and worried about something. Have you followed that child sex-photo thing, Melinda Califona?"

"Followed it? It happened right here in my division. I was flying high, glad we nailed a pair of those bastards, and then somebody moves in and kills the little girl; a warning type execution is all we can figure out. We don't have much to go on."

21

"I'm interested in this one, Kelly. I want to take it right up to the top, whoever he is and wherever. I have a hunch it will take me out of the state in a rush."

"Let's have lunch tomorrow. I'll get together Xerox copies of everything I have, the works."

"Right. I eat lunch early. How about 10:00? I'll call you from near your office and set it up. I'd rather not eat in the department's glorious cafeteria."

"Hey, this one isn't bad. We've got civilians doing the cooking, so it turns out fairly well."

"I'll bet. See you in the morning."

"Yeah, right. Look, keep your cool on this one. Know what I mean? We've heard that there are all sorts of complications on this and even some pressure."

"Big wheels?"

"Who knows? At least we've got almost *zilch* on the killing."

"I'll see you tomorrow."

"Right, I'll do everything I can for you from here."

At precisely 10:00 A.M. Mark called Kelly Patterson from two blocks down the street from the branch sheriff's office building in San Fernando. Five minutes later Captain Kelly, in civilian clothes, walked in the front door of Harry's Coffee Shop with a large envelope under his arm. Kelly looked about the same, a large man with a friendly Irish face now a bit troubled by the burden he carried, but glad to see his longtime friend.

Mark first met Kelly on the original campaign by the Penetrator more years ago than Mark wanted to recall. They had worked on opposite sides for a while, then realized they were both after the same thing and worked together in the wind-up as they quashed a Mafia don and stopped the flow of heroin through one of the pipelines. Ever since then Kelly Patterson had been a covert helper and friend of the Penetrator and one of the few persons in the world who knew exactly who this Penetrator was, or where he could be located.

"Damn, Mark, I wish this one was as easy as it was when we wiped out Don Pietro Scarelli's operation about fifty years ago. This has so many big names floating around, so many bodies turning up, and such a lot of flack that it looks like one for some kind of a major FBI project."

"Sit down, Kelly, and stop griping. Don't try to take away any of my fun. I'm starting to get a feeling about this one and I don't want any competition from the FBI or the Justice Department."

They had shaken hands and sat down and the alert waitress came up for the order. Mark ordered a blood-rare steak and Kelly had a cup of coffee, black. Kelly looked at Mark and scowled.

"You could at least put on some dark glasses. Then the tourists will think you're a movie star. Besides I'm risking my pension sitting here with you. One of the FBI's ten most wanted, aren't you? Here I am consorting with the enemy. What if some young eager beaver deputy spots you and links it up with that composite that came over the wire last month? He sees me having lunch with you. How can I explain that to my chief?"

Mark grinned at him and they got to the business at hand. Kelly knew little more than what the newspapers had printed. The fatal slugs were from a military-type M16-Al, a fully automatic rifle. "The 5.56 mm slugs you know all about from 'Nam," Kelly said. "It looks like a for-hire operation. The car was found a mile away, stolen, and wiped clean. Two men were involved: one drove, and one sat in the back seat with the window down. They knew who the girl was, where she

23

lived, what route she used to walk to school, and when she would be there."

"Your vice people have any other links with nudist clubs, sunshine camps, sex orgies, swap clubs, dirty-picture mills, anything that might tie in?"

"We thought we had something. A woman who lives in the same neighborhood is a friend of the Califonas. Turns out she introduced John to the man who got him into the porn business in the first place; the other guy we nailed. But evidently this Mrs. Berstrom was simply a family friend of both. When my man called on her he recorded the conversation with her approval, and she sounded so rock-solid and pure that we let it alone. The capper is that this Mrs. Berstrom is seventy-seven years old, and a frail, little old lady, with a cook-housekeeper-companion, and a driver-gardener. It just didn't figure she was involved."

Mark nodded. "I see what you mean. Nothing else? No loose ends? No bad vibes anywhere among the Califona family, maybe?"

"Nothing. It's all in here, every lead we tracked down, every citizen complaint about incest and dirty pictures in the whole north county for the past six months. My boys drew a blank."

"Mrs. Berstrom is in there too?"

"Sure." Kelly watched him. "Mark you've got that gleam in your eye again. You're really after this one, aren't you."

"I am. I've read of five or six cases in the last two months all centered around this kiddie porn, and all but one of them ended in a killing. Either we've got two gangs fighting for the business, or one big gun is establishing his territory over the whole U.S. and doing it with a heavy hand."

24

"You find the first wedge into the game, you let me know. I want first crack at anything local, that's got to be a promise. And, Mark, this one I want alive and wrapped up with evidence I can go into court with. If you nail somebody here, this community needs to see justice done, through the courts, the hard way."

The Penetrator nodded. "If at all possible, and if I find a local, I'll tie him with a blue bow for you." Mark grinned. "Captain, why don't you finish your coffee and get back to work. I know it makes you nervous sitting here in public with me so close to all that police power down the street. You've looked at your watch seven times in the past five minutes. Now get out of here."

Kelly closed his eyes and laughed. "You're still the most observant bastard I've ever seen."

"That's how I stay alive. I might be a hunter, but at the same time I'm always one of the ones being hunted. Good-bye, Kelly, I'll keep in touch. And I'll remember the blue ribbon."

Kelly stood, shook hands, turned, and left the restaurant without a backward glance.

Mark's steak hadn't come yet. He motioned to the waitress that he was moving to a larger booth, did so and began going through the papers. When he came to the report on the detective's visit to Mrs. Martha Berstrom, he put it aside and pushed the rest of the papers back into the envelope.

His blood-rare steak came and he ate it, ignoring the mashed potatoes and overcooked vegetables. When the steak was gone, and the glass of ice water empty, he pushed the plate away and read the report.

"From: J. Anderson, Detective. Subject: Mrs. Martha Berstrom. Re: Possible link to pedophile case killing. Subject lives at 1413 Hermosa. House in modest

25

neighborhood, now appreciated in value. Subject seems moderately well off, with two employees to run house and yard.

"M. Berstrom, age 77. Frail yet seemingly in good health. Height about 5–1, white hair. Race: Caucasian. Right-handed. Light-blue eyes, gentle voice. Mrs. Berstrom is a grandmother four times, and a great grandmother twice. Proud of the fact.

"Admitted knowing both John Califona and Tony Marcuso. Marcuso had worked where she worked (LA Hall of Records) before she retired at age 67, ten years ago. She was shocked that either of the men was in trouble with the law.

"Wept when we discussed Melinda Califona. Actual shooting took place only three doors away from Berstrom house. Califonas live about six blocks down the street. Mrs. Berstom did not witness the shooting, since she had not yet got up that morning.

"Subject fed me three kinds of tea while I was there and showed off her four types of indoor orchids. She took two phone calls during the interview. One from the Valley Friends of the Library and one from the Fernando Garden Club.

"Subject strayed from the topic continually, seemed forgetful and had difficulty sometimes following my questions. While not exactly senile, subject did exhibit certain frailties associated with old age.

"Nothing said or done seemed suspicious. The subject was under no emotional strain, showed no nervousness. I found no positive links in any way with the killing, or with the pedophile case."

Mark read it once more, slowly, memorizing the facts and names, then put the file with the others and paid his tab. The Penetrator went outside and drove the Brown Beast, his desert-tested Ford pickup with the small camper on its back, away from the curb and cruised toward the neighborhood where Mrs. Berstrom lived. He had to start somewhere. Anything was better than sitting and trying to come up with leads out of nowhere.

First he would do a minor stakeout on the house, and see what developed. He had everything he needed in the cab of the pickup. Binoculars, canned cola, crackers, even a jar of snacking cheese. If it didn't produce anything else, he would get in a small after-brunch snack.

Mark parked four houses away from the address for Mrs. Berstrom and on the same side of the street. It was a middle-class neighborhood with touches of grandeur. No cars parked on the street. All houses had double garages, nice lawns. He parked, slid a straw hat down over his eyes, but left a slit where he could see out, and pretended to be sleeping.

The Penetrator watched the house for two hours and nothing happened. No one went in or came out. He really didn't expect anyone to, but it was worth a shot. Now he would use the direct approach, the cold-shower technique.

Mark left the camper, crossed the street, walked past the house, and came back to it from the other direction. He had dressed that morning in a blue turtleneck knit shirt, dark blue pants, and a lightweight sport coat. That should be dressy enough to go calling.

As he walked up the drive, Mark put together his strategy and his opening lines.

Mrs. Berstrom herself opened the door when he rang

the bell. She was exactly like the report indicated, everyone's sweet, little, fragile grandmother with a winning smile.

"Mrs. Berstrom?"

"Yes, but I'm not buying anything."

"Good, because I'm not selling. This will only take a minute, and I'll tell you right here. I'm from the committee and frankly members of the committee are unhappy with the way you've been handling things in your area. The laws here are fairly relaxed, but we can't afford to flout them, or to get any publicity. You've been doing too much of both. We realize you had no direct involvement in the silencing of the Califona girl, but those people who did must have been in your area-committee sequencing. The central committee intends only to warn you this time."

"I don't have the slightest idea what you're talking about."

"Good, I like that attitude. Remember, we just give one warning, and only one. You've made your one allowable mistake. Don't make another one."

Mark paused and watched her. The confidence, the supreme in-command presence she exhibited when she first came to the door slipped, then it crumbled slowly, and stark fear came into her eyes. Mark knew he had selected the right starting point. While the fear was still there, raw and chilling her, he turned and walked away without another word.

He felt her eyes on him as he went, but he never looked back. He walked directly past the brown pickup and to the corner, and then turned so the woman couldn't see him anymore, if she were still watching. He waited for two minutes by his watch, took off the light-blue sport coat and turned it inside out so it became a light-brown one. He put on a small billed cap from the

28

coat pocket and walked slowly back to the brown pickup, stepped inside, and sat down to wait.

He watched Mrs. Berstrom's house. The lady would not trust the telephone with this kind of message. She might call and ask for someone to come over, or she might go somewhere herself. Either way, Mark knew he had a small handle on the child-porno game. He had a beginning and he wouldn't stop until he blasted this filthy racket into a million pieces.

CHAPTER 3

A Blue Ribbon Special

Less than ten minutes after Mark left the Berstrom home, he saw a blue Pontiac back out of the garage; the big door closed automatically and the Pontiac rolled down the street away from him. There was a man behind the wheel and he saw the white head of Mrs. Berstrom in the back seat.

Mark let the car get a block ahead, memorized the license plate number, 076-MWW, and followed it. The Pontiac drove straight down Hermosa, then stopped in the 1000 block. No one got out. A moment later a woman came out of a house; she got into the car and it drove away. Mark noted the number of the house, 1014, as he passed. Kelly could help him there.

Mark drove carefully behind the Pontiac, never getting closer then one block. He didn't think the driver would be looking for a tail, but if he did, the Brown Beast would be spotted almost at once. He hung back, barely making contact, knowing the other driver could lose him in a few sudden turns if he tried. But the man ahead evidently wasn't watching, which meant he wasn't worried about a shadow.

After four miles of winding through residential streets, the blue Pontiac came into the business section of the city of San Fernando and parked in a lot at the side of a store named THE CAMPING PLACE, "Everything for the Sportsman."

The two women went in a side door. The driver checked the Pontiac door, then looked at the tires before he followed them into the store.

Mark parked in the far end of the same lot and got into the camper, where he changed clothes quickly, putting on jeans, a cotton flannel shirt, a blue baseball-type bill cap with FORD on the front of it, and a pair of silver reflecting sunglasses. Even if Mrs. Berstrom bumped into him now she wouldn't recognize him. When he got inside the store, the driver was still there looking at a display of handguns, but Mark did not see the two women anywhere in the store.

There was no other side door, just the main ones, and the way the driver was walking around, it looked like the women were in the store somewhere. Mark checked out the saltwater fishing gear at a counter.

"Hey, man. Those Salas 8's any good for yellowtail? I wanted to jig off the bottom, or maybe do some fast retrieves from 'way down deep."

The clerk frowned, then shrugged. "We got them, but I'm not the fishing man. I don't know what works out there."

"Thanks for the help," Mark growled and the clerk left. It gave the Penetrator time to look around. The store was big, with masses of hunting and fishing gear, as well as equipment for all of the team sports—shoes, uniforms, equipment, the works. At the back a stairway led to a second floor where a series of offices opened off a hallway. Evidently that was where the business side of the operation was.

Mark looked at a few more items, then went out the front door and spotted a phone booth half a block down. He punched up Kelly Patterson's number at the sheriff's office.

"Kelly, I've got a new address for you to check out," he told Kelly when the cop picked up the phone. "It's 1014 Hermosa, just down the street from your favorite grandmother. Find out anything you can for me about the people there, especially a woman in her forties."

"This tie-in with the kiddie-porn thing?" Kelly asked.

"I sure hope so. Also did you do a complete background check on our grandmother friend? It might pay to dig out everything you can find on her. I talked to her today and she was so scared by the time I left she could have killed me. Then five minutes later she took off on a dead run and picked up this woman at the address I gave you. She's scared and looking for some help and I hope leading us to the next rung up this ladder. I'll get back to you as soon as I have anything more. That is a part of your blue ribbon."

"Berstrom, I'll be damned. That nice little old grandmother . . ."

"Yeah, and she may be head over heels in the pedophilia racket right in your own backyard. I've got to move. I'll keep in touch."

He walked to the edge of the sporting goods store and looked in the parking lot. The blue Pontiac was still in the same slot. He had some time to kill. He looked up and down the street and about a block down he saw something that interested him. A large sign proclaimed: ADULT BOOKSTORE. He grinned, crossed the street, and walked to the place. A sign in the window said: "No one under 18 allowed inside."

It had been a long time since he had scouted a good, dirty bookstore. Before he went inside he looked back at the sports store; neither of the women he had followed had come out.

Inside he squeezed past a half-dozen men reading the covers of the books. The cover pictures and art were all suggestive, all showed at least half a naked woman. A sign over the racks said: ABSOLUTELY NO READING. "You Read It, You Bought It!" In back another sign said: NO SITTING OR SQUATTING ALLOWED! Over another section the sign read KEEP YOUR HANDS OUT OF YOUR POCKETS!

A reject from the LA Rams' line lumbered through the narrow aisles staring hard at everyone. Muscles bulged under his T-shirt, which was labeled in front and in back with one word: BOUNCER!

Mark found what he was most interested in at the back. The books were in front, then the more flagrant skin magazines, and last on the shelves the homosexual magazines, together with those for other far-out persuasions. On one rack a dozen copies of *Life Child* were displayed. The cover showed twin white girls about ten, naked, sitting on a velvet couch, with their hands folded demurely at their crotches. The price on the cover was fifteen dollars. Mark picked it up and walked back to the cashier.

He paid for the magazine. "Hey, where in hell does a guy find some of this kind of action around here?" Mark said, indicating the magazine cover. The male clerk took his money, ignored the question, put the magazine in a brown envelope, and stapled the top. The clerk moved away as though he hadn't even heard Mark.

Behind him Mark heard a guffaw.

"Hey, man, you ain't gonna get no names and places

33

in here, that's for damn sure. You know why? You look too damn much like an undercover cop, that's why!"

Mark looked at a thin black of about twenty-two or -three, who grinned at him.

"Yeah, I think you're right," Mark said. "Hey, you know?"

The young black shook his head, and walked back into the stacks of sex books.

The Penetrator went out to the street and walked quickly to where he could see the parking lot in back of the sports store. The blue Pontiac was not there. Mark worried it for a minute. Then he was sure. Grandma Berstrom had panicked, headed for help. She wouldn't stop here unless this was where she could get some help or get calmed down. This must have been the next link in the chain, and he would check it out.

Mark climbed in the back of the camper and looked at the magazine. It was terrible. *Life Child* was more explicit than he had bargained for but he had seen worse. There was no masthead, no indication of who published or printed the book. That way no one could trace it back to its source.

He put the magazine in a file drawer under the sink and checked his watch. It was just after 3:00. Mark lay down on the bunk and programmed himself for a two-hour nap. He relaxed and was sleeping within thirty seconds. Intense concentration would wake him up precisely at 5:00 P.M.

When he got up at 5:00, Mark looked at his canned food supply, picked out a can of chili with hamburger, heated it on his butane stove, and soon had a poor man's chili size with chopped onions and cheese. Tomato juice topped it off, and when he looked outside the next time, it was almost dark.

Mark drove the camper out of the parking lot and

34

down the street half a mile to a phone booth, where he dialed Kelly. The cop was still working.

"You taking two shifts?" Mark asked.

"Had a little action here. I'll be around until nine or ten tonight."

"What did you come up with on that address?"

"A surprise. That's where Tony Marcuso lived before he went into the slammer with Califona. It must have been his wife that Mrs. Berstrom picked up. So maybe Marcuso's wife was in on it too. We're still working on your grandmother."

"There's got to be something on her somewhere, maybe way back. I may get in touch with you later tonight, Kelly."

"More blue ribbons?"

"I hope so. I'm waiting for it to get dark."

"A little breaking and entering?"

"Usually no breaking is required, just a little climbing."

"Look, Mark, be careful. Some of these San Fernando city cops are sharp. I can't help you if one of them nails you halfway into somebody's window."

"Forget it, they'll never see me. I'll keep in touch."

They hung up and Mark went into the back of the camper and changed into his night work clothes: tight-fitting black pants, soft sponge-rubber soled shoes, a black, long-sleeved T-shirt with pouches in front and back, and a black watch cap.

For a half-hour the Penetrator went over the files Kelly had given him on the Califona killing and the porno case. He found nothing he had missed. Mrs. Berstrom still looked like the only lead he had. If there were a connection between any of these kiddie-porn activities, this might be a place to get into the network. The bigger the network, the more chances for slipups, the more chance that someone might leave vital information around where it shouldn't be. He was counting on that.

It was dark by 6:30. Mark drove the camper to within half a block of the sports store and parked on the same side of the street. The store had closed at 6:00 and the night lights were on, but no lights showed on the second-floor offices. A quick walk along the alley side of the long building showed one second-story window cracked open.

Mark did as he had done so many times before, climbing up the vertical side of the building like a human fly, finding crevices and bulges and crooks in the stucco that most people would overlook to put his hands and feet in. It took him only three minutes to get up the side of the two-story building and to the open window. This was the dangerous time, when he might be spotted and had little means of defense. He leaned inside the window and then stepped in and pulled the window closed. Just then a San Fernando city police car cruised slowly through the alley, spotlight checking the rear doors of each business.

Mark was in an office. Using a pencil flash he looked it over quickly and found only sporting goods-related records.

He moved to another office and found the same. The owner's large carpeted office was next; he skipped it and went through a connecting door into the upper level of the back part of the store. It was over the stockroom below and at one time must have been used for stock as well. Now one of the larger rooms had been turned into a photo studio. It had a ten-foot-high ceiling, and a dozen expensive studio lights stood on stands and hung on an iron pipe high against the ceiling.

Mark looked farther. The next door was locked. He

opened the lock in forty-five seconds using picks from his pocket. This room was smaller and contained records and files. On the desk lay a paper that said: "Shooting Schedule" on top. The next session was set for 8:00 P.M. that same night. Mark dug into files and boxes and soon had what he wanted. Negative files that showed pedophile poses. Hundreds of them.

He went through the desk, minutely, looking for anything that might tie in this operation with some other one. It was an inside office with no outside window, so he turned on the lights and checked every file and desk drawer in the room. Almost half an hour later he found it. A letter deep in a file marked "Correspondence." It was a letterhead from the International Pedophilia League, but there were no names or addresses on it. That was a start and a new element in the puzzle.

Mark searched for twenty minutes more, then took out the writing boards that pulled out from each side of the desk. On the bottom of each was a sheet of paper with a list of names and addresses. They were neatly taped in place and with a current date in the upper left-hand corner not more than a month old. The top name on the list of sixty names and addresses was circled in red ink. It had a Los Angeles address.

Mark used his knife, slit the tape, and took off both sheets of paper, folded them, and put them in his back pocket. He had a start on what he needed. He was at the hallway about to check another office when he heard a key turn in a lock at the head of the long hall. Voices sounded and someone laughed.

The Penetrator darted back to the first office he had been in, opened the window, and eased out into space. He closed the window after glancing both ways along the alley, then quickly worked down the side of the wall to the alley and walked to his pickup. On the way he

37

passed a phone booth and, smiling, he stopped and phoned Captain Kelly Patterson.

"Kelly, I've got the rest of that blue ribbon for you. Get your people and probably San Fernando Police to the Camping Place on Fourth, a sporting goods store. Upstairs in back there's a photo studio and all the pedophilic negatives and pictures you'll need. I just saw some people going in there and it looks like a photo session is starting. You'll know how to coordinate a hit."

"You're not fooling me? It's the porno place?"

"All wrapped up with blue ribbon, buddy. If you rush it."

Mark walked on to the Brown Beast, got in and drove to the far side of the street, and parked more than a block down from the Camping Place and headed away from it. A car Mark guessed was an unmarked city-cop rig slid into position by the front door. Another one parked near the side door. Ten minutes later there were more than a dozen police cars and sheriff's units around the store.

Silently a two-man SWAT team slid around the building and forced the side door. Ten more SWAT team members rose from hidden positions and charged noiselessly through the door.

A few police slipped inside the store, Captain Patterson among them. The muffled shot came as a surprise, then a window broke on the second floor and a man leaped out. Two police were there when he hit. The jumper broke one leg and a wrist in the fall. Mark drove around until he found an all-night drugstore and copied the two pages of names and addresses on a Xerox machine, then went back toward the sports store.

Two dozen police cars were there now, and Mark parked and walked up, asking the first sheriff's deputy

38

if he knew where Captain Patterson was. The man shook his head, then pointed.

"Hey, you're in luck. There he is, just getting into that command car."

The pastel Ford's engine had started when Mark tapped on the window. Kelly rolled down the glass and saw Mark, said something to the driver, and jumped out. His grin took up half his face.

"Caught them with their pants down, good buddy! Thanks. Everybody in the studio was mother naked including the photographer and the makeup girl. We've got enough on all of them to put them away for years. Except the three kids; we sent them home. The mother of the little girl was there, too. Can you believe that?"

"I'm beginning to believe almost anything, Kelly. Have you ever heard of the International Pedophilia League?"

"You mean there *is* such an animal?"

"Seems to be." He took out the originals of the lists and handed them to Kelly. "Those were taped under the pull boards on the desk up there. Haven't looked at them carefully, but most of the addresses seem to be out of town. It might tie in."

"You were upstairs here then before?"

"Just a short visit. There didn't seem to be anybody home, so I left," Mark grinned. "And you found all the pedophilia pictures you need for convictions?"

"Plenty. We've got them all with the blue ribbon."

"Oh, sit on the list for a couple of days, will you? I want to look over some of the names, especially that one in Los Angeles."

"Hell, yes. Easy. I've got enough to keep me busy for a week right here. I've got to help get these people booked."

Kelly got back in his car after a firm handshake. "Hey, buddy, anytime you find some more blue ribbon, remember your friends."

"Right, I'll do that," Mark said and watched the police car drive away.

CHAPTER 4

Hollywood Party Time

It was ten o'clock the morning after the San Fernando bust when Mark found the address he wanted on Sunset Boulevard in Los Angeles. The one-story, stucco building had a fresh coat of paint, sun awnings over the windows in front, and a new-looking sign above the door that read: McMILLEN ENTERPRISES, "Motion Pictures." Mark drove on past and found a phone booth.

"Paul McMillen, please." Mark said when a voice answered.

"Thank you," the operator said. Someone picked up the phone on the third ring.

"McMillen here."

"Mr. Paul McMillen?"

"Speaking."

"Mr. McMillen, you've never met me. I'm Arnie from New York, and I'm in town for just a few days. I was told that you and I are in the same league, and I thought you might be able to recommend some, what shall we say, some special entertainment."

The gruff businesslike voice from the other end of the line mellowed and relaxed. "Well, yes, of course. Hey, I'm glad you called. Always glad to help out a new friend. Those of us in the league certainly do have to help each other. I've done traveling, and I know what it's like to be in a strange town all alone. If you're free right now, why don't we have a cup of coffee somewhere. How about the Inn Place. That's with two *n*'s. It's not far from my business on Sunset. It's in the 7800 block. I always prefer to talk in person rather than on the phone."

"Yes, good idea. I'll find the spot. Say in half an hour?"

"Excellent, Arnie. I'll see you there, at about 10:30."

When he hung up Mark smiled grimly, walked back to his camper, and got in the back. He changed clothes, putting on his $350 executive suit, one of his narrow ties, and combed his black hair. Then he added three dashes of Aramis cologne, and checked the building numbers. He was within a block of the Inn Place, so he walked.

It turned out to be a bit awkward contacting the right man. There was no hostess to leave a name with. Mark watched several single men come in and guessed the wrong one each time. McMillen was five minutes late. At last Mark just sat back in the booth and waited for the man to find him.

He came a moment later, smiling and relaxed. Paul McMillen was a slight man, about forty, with a golden suntan, dyed black hair, an expensive suit and $150 shoes. A gold chain connected the pockets of his vest and a Phi Beta Kappa key hung from the center. Mark instinctively disliked the man, perhaps for knowing

42

what he was. The Penetrator waved him into the booth and held out his hand.

"Hi, I'm Johnson, Arnie Johnson. I don't think I gave you my full name on the phone. I like to be a little careful about that."

McMillen sat down, his smile widening. "Oh, yes, I know what you mean. We have to be damn careful. Right out in the Valley last night we had some trouble. They raided a store and barged in on a photo session. And that on private property and out of sight, if you can imagine that. The whole thing probably will be thrown out of court because they didn't even have a search warrant as I understand it. At least that's what the paper said. But then you can never believe much you read in the newspapers anymore." He grinned now and Mark noticed the expensive capped teeth with a hint of gold behind some.

"Say, I like your suit," McMillen said. "Is that one from the new Johnny Carson line? He makes suits now you know, and they're not bad at all."

"I'm not much on labels, Mr. McMillen."

"Hey, this is California. None of that mister stuff. I'm Paul, just call me Paul."

"Thanks. I'm Arnie. I don't have a lot of time, can you help me?"

"Yes, of course, Arnie. I make it a rule always to meet my new friends in the league, and talk and then decide. Once about three years ago we had some trouble with the vice squad trying to infiltrate; so now we are a little paranoid, but a lot more secure. The cops are as crooked as the crooks these days, but we have to live with them." He watched Mark for a moment. "And I wanted to remind you that this is sunny California. I mean, some folks out here are a little more relaxed and laid back. They like to go two or even three different

43

ways, if you understand. I don't want you to get upset or surprised if that happens to you. We're a lot more broad-minded than most of you Easterners. Lots of times our people look for some kind of a trade-off, you know: I help you out and you do something for me."

Mark signaled the waitress. He had been fidgeting and nervous-acting like he hoped a hard-up pedophile might. McMillen grinned.

"You're a little jumpy, aren't you? Well, I've got something that should take care of you. Just the thought of her. She's an eight-year-old blonde, a real little sweetheart and not scared or shy at all, if you know what I mean." His voice dropped down several tones now, and he stopped when the waitress came up. Mark ordered another cup of coffee and asked for one for McMillen.

"Usually when I'm talking about my favorite subject this way, I never get into liquor or even caffeine. I want nothing to deaden my senses for such a delicious outing." As he talked his blue eyes were darting and alive. "Oh, this small blonde comes in a package with a larger-type blonde mother, who is about thirty-two or thirty-three, a real winner, a knockout who is one of the multiple types I was telling you about. Any sexual combinations you can come up with are great with her. She digs salt and pepper, but that won't be a factor here."

Mark shifted in his seat, looked around, nervously. Then took a handkerchief from his pocket and dabbed his forehead.

Paul McMillen smiled. "Hey, take it easy, Arnie. Nothing to worry about. The owner here is one of our people. He sets up lots of things for us. He's got some wild back rooms, too, that we use from time to time; but it takes a group for that and we don't have any groups scheduled for a while."

"I was hoping for something with a crowd. I dig the

44

watching part too," Mark said, letting his voice drop so low McMillen could hardly hear him. "Yeah, and I'd like to get in on some of those crazy photo sessions I've heard about."

McMillen shook his head a bit grimly. "After that photo bust in the Valley last night, there won't be that kind of action around here for quite a while. Fact is that was the only real professional studio our people had in this whole area. Might be some smaller ones, but those jokers in the Valley had ties right on up to the top."

"Damn. They said there was lots of action out here. The folks in New York are going to be disappointed. I've even got some great coke to share."

McMillen shook his head. "Wrong league, man. When we're onto something good, most of us like to keep straight. The drug scene is a real bummer; you can't remember a damn thing the next day—at least I can't, and for me that's half the kicks, the memories."

"What about a pair of eleven-year-old girls?" Mark asked quietly, deliberately looking away from Paul as he did so.

McMillen sipped at the coffee in front of him. "Well, that's getting a little old for us on the Coast. More available is the seven- to eight-year-old range out here. Parents are younger and the kids don't really care that much. But eleven, wow. Some of them are getting horny themselves by then, especially the girls. Eleven is just too old." He sat there a minute, tapping a thirty-dollar mechanical pencil made from mahogany on the booth table top. Mark sipped at his coffee.

"Tell you what. I've got a little get-together planned at my place tonight . . ."

"Oh, no. I couldn't impose. I've got to see these two

45

producers today about a new circuit we're setting up, and then I'm going to be all wrung out."

McMillen sat up straighter. "New circuit? Are you a distributor? You work for a distributor?"

"Yes, Prometheus Distribution. We like to steal a little bit of heaven and give it back to men."

"You're really playing with fire that way."

They both laughed at their little joke.

McMillen leaned forward. "Did you know that I'm a producer? McMillen Enterprises."

"Is that so? Well I didn't mean to imply that we handled anything big. I mean, we're a small outfit so far, and we distribute short subjects and some documentaries to art theaters and some of the Theater-Four places that are trying to build slightly longer programs for their audiences. We're small, but growing. Right now we have about one hundred and thirty theaters."

McMillen laughed and rubbed one hand over his face. "Strange what a small world it is, Arnie. I'm not a big-shot feature producer. I do mostly documentaries, and a short now and then. Looks just like the type of distributor I've been hunting for. We'll have to talk a lot more. I insist that you come to my place tonight at 5:30 for some early drinks and we'll talk. There might be some other small producers there you'd like to meet. Right now, if you have time, I want you to come down to my office and I'll show you some of the films we produce. I think you'll like them."

Mark tried to look surprised. "Well, all right, but I can't promise you anything, you understand that." He frowned. "Oh, and I didn't mean to imply that we could use anything other then purely straight, square film. You know, no stag movies or anything that is porn or pedophilia."

"Right, no porn. I realize that, Arnie. Hey, I do some great stuff that I'm proud of."

"Strictly business," Mark said firmly. "I don't mix business judgments, pleasure, or friendship."

McMillen nodded. "You bet. My work is good. It's going to knock your eyes out. As soon as we finish here, you get the guided tour and you're going to like it."

Mark took the walk through McMillen Enterprises. It was mostly offices for the producer, with one small photo studio for publicity stills. He sat through two fifteen-minute documentaries and made the required comments. There were some parts of the studio they did not go into. With McMillen's inclination toward kinky sex, Mark figured the chances were almost one-hundred percent that he was also shooting a few pedophilic movies on the side. He'd have to come back and check that out. If the two-bit producer were, it might be a spot where a link could be found between this peanuts operation and "all the way to the top," as McMillen had put it.

Mark toured the bookshops along Hollywood and Sunset Strip the rest of the afternoon and found numerous titles in the kiddy porn and pedophile field, but always *Life Child* was prominently displayed. It seemed to be the top seller in the field.

Mark arrived at the Beverly Hills home at exactly 5:30 and McMillen was on the sidewalk to greet him. Mark knew none of the people at the party except the host. The guests were on the fringes of the Hollywood scene, some from feature films and productions, but mostly into documentary work. The blonde with the bombshell daughter did not show up, and Mark felt he was wasting his time. He made one more circuit and was heading for the door when a girl came in, kissed McMillen on the cheek, and gave him her wrap. She was a striking brunet, a compact five-feet four with a remarkably beautiful face, and a slender figure with big breasts. She wore a sleek golden dress that clung to her like a wet T-shirt, thin shoulder straps holding up the plunging neckline top. Mark stopped and stared. She smiled, watching him. Paul McMillen said something to her and she walked straight to Mark, where she reached up and kissed his cheek. Her perfume was serious.

"Hello, we don't believe in formal introductions out here in California. I'm Drisana." Her voice was stronger, lower than he'd expected. When he said nothing she smiled and went on. "You're an extremely handsome man, except when you let your mouth fall open that way, staring at people. Usually it's not polite to stare so hard, but in this case, you're forgiven."

Mark reached for her hand and held it. He chuckled, and shook his head, then glanced down at the girl's face.

"Then I'm not dreaming. I've been nodding off now and then at this little fling, and when you came, poured so delightfully into that scrap of a dress, I was sure I'd died and gone straight to heaven."

Drisana laughed softly. "Well, you are alive, after all. And thank you for the nice compliments. But I still don't know your name."

"Oh, Arnie. I'm Arnie Johnson, from New York. I'm in film distribution."

"Damn! Well, it figures. At last I meet a knockout of a man and he's from New York. How long are you gong to be in town?"

"A few days," Mark laughed. "I'm afraid I'm not used to saying thank yous for compliments. I'm out of my depth here, but thank you anyway." He took her hand and looped it through his arm and held onto it. "Can I get you a drink?"

"Perrier," she said. "It's all I drink."

"I'm not going to let go of you, so let's find the bar that's the longest walk from here."

It was on the patio, where Chinese paper lanterns ringed the cement slab that had been covered with green outdoor carpet. The pool looked inviting and half a dozen were swimming. All but one had on a swimsuit, and the naked girl was more than a little drunk. One man was trying to get her out of the pool.

Mark and Drisana wandered around the backyard, then sat on a cement bench near some gloriously blooming deep-red bougainvillea with a border of bird-of-paradise plants.

"Are you in the business?" Mark asked.

"What business? Show business or the film business?"

"Either."

"Both," she said.

"And you're a big talker now that I've got you started, Drisana. I'm not up on my ethnic names. Where does such a pretty name come from?"

"Actually it's Sanskrit and means daughter of the sun. If one of my parents was the sun, I don't know who my other one was, maybe Pluto or Alpha Centauri, I'm not sure. My friends shorten it to Drisa. That's pronounced Dree-SAH." Her soft brown eyes glowed up at him. "Wow!" Are you sure you're not a movie star in some big, hairy movie?"

"Sorry, just in my other incarnation, but I don't go into that."

They talked and walked and chatted with other people for an hour, and Mark was ready to chalk it up as an interesting evening with a beautiful girl, but he had learned nothing that would help him with the pedophile problem. The only thing he could think of was to get back in the studio, check out the place and see if McMillen was as pristine pure as he claimed. And Mark needed to find a tie-in, the next step up the ladder. Curiously he figured this was the best shot he'd had at it so far.

Drisa was more than cooperative. She never left his side. She barely spoke to anyone else, nodding and waving, but not leaving him. They were outside in the warm California evening, just off the patio near two tall tree ferns, when he leaned over and kissed her soft lips. She looked up, surprised, then he saw pleasure wreathe her lovely face.

"Would you care to try that again without sneaking up on a girl?"

He took her in his arms and kissed her again. This time she responded, holding him tightly, pushing her breasts hard against his chest, pressing closely with her body all the way down.

He came away from her lips slowly. "Now that was fine," he said. "I think it's time we leave the party."

"I've been waiting a half-hour for you to say that: Paul always has lousy parties. I told him I could jazz it up for him a little, but he said no. I'll get my wrap and see you at the front door in about two minutes."

Mark found Paul McMillen and bowed out, saying that he had to go but that he would call him the next day.

At the door, Mark waited, thinking it through. He had stayed alive by not doing the obvious, by not being trapped by the easy snare. When Drisa came she looked a little too smug, too satisfied.

"Your car or mine?" she asked.

"Mine," he said. "Your place or mine?"

"Mine," she said. "I'll show you where it is."

Wrong, thought Mark as he guided her down the sidewalk to his pickup. She giggled when she saw it.

"Now this is wild! You bring your own loving pad to the party! Out of sight. Let's get in the back. I want to see it!"

"Later, not here. We have to cruise out of here first, then we'll have the guided tour back there."

He drove. She asked him twice when they were going to stop. She sat very close to him, her leg touching his, her hand on his leg.

"Let's stop here, this is a good place," she said without looking out the window.

A mile farther on he did stop, and when she looked out she found they were on a side street near Hollywood.

"Hey, why are we stopping here? Cops work past this area."

"First we talk. You work for McMillen. Why was I your target for tonight?"

"Work for McMillen? I hardly know the man."

"Don't deny it, Drisa. You came in, saw me, McMillen told you I was the one, and you never glanced at anybody else all night. I've heard enough snow jobs to see through your poor one. What I want to know is why?"

"He told me to be nice to you, and to see that you have a good time. Is there anything illegal about that? You're a distributor and he hopes you can use some of his films—so I am nice to you."

"That's all?"

"Maybe all for him. Me, I'm interested in more personal things." She rubbed higher on his leg.

He ignored the move. "Do you have a key to the McMillen offices? They're just around the corner."

"No, I don't."

51

"Have you ever appeared in any of his films?"

"What? Oh, yes, sometimes. I narrated one for him."

"Undressed?"

"No, it was a documentary."

"No porno films, no pedophilia stuff?"

"Of course not!"

"Come on, we're going to pay a call on McMillen Enterprises, through the side door."

The side door lock took Mark almost a minute to pick, then they were inside. They went to McMillen's office and Mark searched quickly, expertly. On the underside of the desk pullout board he found nothing. The desk revealed only legitimate business material. They looked further and for some reason Drisa seemed willing to help him.

Mark tried Drisa again. "Look, I know McMillen shoots pornographic films at his studios, and I know you were in some of them. I recognize you from at least one of them. So why try to lie your way out of it? Maybe I can help get you off with the judge."

"Judge? You some kind of cop?"

"No, but before I'm through here cops will be all over the place. I can leave you tied up as witness number one."

"No, no, don't do that. I saw that film about women's prisons. I couldn't take that."

"So talk. You've been in his porn films?"

"Yes."

"Some of the child-sex things too?"

"One, only one; then I told him no more."

"He keep the stuff around here?"

"Yes. Hell, I might as well show you, you'll find them anyway. Down in the film room."

She led the way. In one cabinet, past double locks, Mark found master prints of the porn reels. "My Favorite Boy," was one. Another was "Two Little Girls and Me." They were half-hour 16-mm films.

"Well now, look at this," Mark said, holding up a clipboard. On it were mailing labels made out to Multimedia, Inc., c/o Air Freight Forwarding Office. COD, Honolulu, Hawaii.

"Have you heard of this place before?" he asked.

"Yes. Paul ships his stuff there. They get a first shipment of four hundred copics."

"What is Multimedia, a distributor?"

"Yes, at least that. Paul has done business with them for over two years."

"Let's see what else we can find." In a book he found a record of shipments to the firm covering the past two years. Each film had a number and a code name. In the same locked drawer he discovered a correspondence file. One letter must have been sent with each shipment. There were twenty or thirty of them, but only two letters that had come back. Both were on plain letter-sized newsprint paper. The paper would be impossible to trace. There was no letterhead, both notes were typed. One said simply: "Received shipment, four hundred prints of #14P-12, Charlie. Check enclosed." The initials on the letter were P.M.

Mark looked for the original A & B rolls, the vital parts of the film used for final master prints, but coudn't find them. The masters evidently were not there either. For a moment Mark sat in a chair staring at the pedophilic material.

"If movie film burned as well as it used to, we'd have no problem," Mark said. He took out a dozen of the porno films and scattered them around the room. Then he ran back to the pickup, found a thermite grenade in the weapons section, and ran back inside the office.

"You're really going to burn down the place?" Drisa asked.

"Why not? At least it will give the Los Angeles fire Department some practice, and it will bring cops by the dozen, so your little buddy Paul McMillen will be out of business."

The door to the film room slammed open and McMillen stood there, a small automatic in his hand.

"Not out of business, Arnie. You and the traitor there are the ones out of business. You'll both be found dead out in the Valley somewhere, a murder-suicide. Of course Drisa's clothes will be torn off and that beautiful body messed up."

Mark stared at the gun. Probably a .32, nothing larger. He could absorb one shot and still knock down McMillen, if the round didn't hit him in a vital area. It would be a last-resort try. What else could he do? Stall him? Try to psych him out?

"It won't matter, McMillen. You're through. I've sent copies of four of the films to the police vice squad by messenger. He just left. Vice will have them in a half-hour and then you're a dead duck. You're finished, McMillen. You wouldn't let it alone. Why didn't you stick to the documentaries? Some of them were pretty good."

"Don't try to con me, Arnie. You haven't been into the locked vault that long. The alarm went off just twenty-five minutes ago. I roared right down here."

Mark watched McMillen. He was serious. His hand steady. He whispered to Drisana. "Distract him, strip or something."

Mark hooked his thumbs in his belt and watched McMillen. The .45 was inches away under the jacket front in the clip-on holster at Mark's right side.

"Before you murder us in cold blood, McMillen,

why Hawaii? Evidently there's some kind of a whole-saler there, but why not Chicago, more centrally located."

McMillen laughed. "Hawaii is where the whole ball of wax is, man. That's where the printing is done on the magazine, books, posters, and pictures. Everything but the films, which I take care of. The sex devices, the gimmicks, everything else comes together there for shipments. I was there a year ago, fantastic operation."

Drisa had pushed one golden strap of the clinging dress off her shoulder and the top of the dress sagged, slipped downward, showing one large pink-tipped breast.

McMillen saw it and scowled. "That won't work, Drisa. I've seen it all before. You sold out on me. I can't allow that. This time you've gone too far."

Mark watched him glance at her breast, stare back at him, then flick his eyes at the girl again. Mark timed the movement perfectly; his hand stabbed for the .45, pulled it clear and he dove for the floor, rolled, and came up shooting. He heard two shots before he got off his two rounds, but felt no pain. His first shot sliced McMillen's right leg; his second hit Paul's shoulder and spun him around, blasting the gun from his hand and jolting him backward against the door casing. There he slid slowly to the floor, groaning, holding his injured shoulder.

Mark picked up the small automatic and put it in his belt, holstered his own .45, then carried McMillen to the front of the building. There he snapped on plastic, notched riot cuffs hand and foot and sat McMillen in a chair. At a typewriter he wrote out this note:

"Dear LAPD: Here is one Paul McMillen, slightly punctured pornographer and pedophilic filmmaker. This place is part of a pedophilia network. You'll find

55

plenty of evidence in the rear. Put this one out of circulation for a long time."

Mark put the note on the desk and placed two authentic chipped blue-flint arrowheads on top of it, then turned to McMillen.

"Now, the address in Honolulu. Where does this stuff wind up, and what's the man's name?"

McMillen laughed, then swore at Mark until his face turned white and he passed out. His shoulder was bleeding badly. Mark found some tape and cloth and put a compress over the bullet holes, so he wouldn't bleed to death. He wanted McMillen tried and convicted as a warning to others. It was plain he wasn't going to get any names out of him.

He grabbed the phone and told the police there was a man shot at the Sunset address; they needed an ambulance and the vice squad. Then he hung up quickly, and ran out the side door with Drisa in tow. They drove half a block down Sunset where they could see the business and waited.

Los Angeles police responded in three minutes. Five minutes later a sergeant's supervisor car pulled up and shortly after that, two unmarked cars with plainclothesmen. Vice had arrived.

Mark drove away.

Now all he needed was a name, he had a city.

Drisa pushed up beside him as he drove.

"You're really serious about wanting to stop all that child-sex stuff, aren't you?"

"Deadly serious."

"I might be able to help."

He didn't respond, kept driving, checking traffic.

"Hey, I said I could help. Paul was the biggest supplier of films to Hawaii. In fact he had copies made of films he didn't produce. He promised to take me over there but he didn't. He even mentioned the guy's name he worked with once, and I'm trying to remember it. Would that help—if I could remember the name? You can't get nothing from that COD at the airport. I mean how are you going to arrest an address in care of air freight?"

Mark glanced at her. "Yes, the name would help. Think hard, and remember I didn't leave you back there for the cops. I'll also make it worth your while.

"Hey, I don't want money."

"What would help you remember?"

"Well, my job is finished. I don't work for Mr. McMillen anymore. I'm at liberty." She put her hand on his leg again. "I'm free to travel . ... to Hawaii?"

"And you want a nice trip to the Islands?"

"Well, if I can help, if I can remember the name. I already helped you find the film, and to distract Paul when he had the gun. Doesn't that count?"

"Yes, Drisa." As he drove he knew the name would save him a lot of time, days and days of digging-time. "Okay, you remember it and you've got a two-way ticket to Hawaii."

"Good." She smiled at him. "I remember things best early in the mornings, after I wake up. I need to sleep on it."

"Where should I take you?"

"Anywhere we can park overnight. I don't want to be alone tonight. I want to spend it with you in your camper—and you haven't given me the guided tour yet."

CHAPTER 5

Pedophile Phonemanship

Mark slept halfway through the 2,500-mile flight from Los Angeles to Honolulu. He woke up only when Drisana pulled at his sleeve.

"There's a good movie on. *South Pacific!*" she said, excitement spilling through her voice. "You want to watch it?"

"I've seen it," Mark said and tried to get back to sleep in the tilt-back airline seat, but it was useless. She looked at him and smiled.

"Hey, I thought you were going to sleep all day. Isn't this just a super flight!"

Mark was fully awake now. He turned and watched Drisa, the girl who knew the missing name in Hawaii—if she could remember it. She wore a white-and-green blouse that he swore was a size too small, showing off her figure remarkably well. A tight green skirt ending just below her knees and a light-green kerchief tied around her throat finished her traveling costume. She had checked two suitcases. Mark had known all along that she was a gamble, but he had counted her as a calculated risk that he could handle. If she came up with the name to go with the business firm, he would be days ahead.

"Think of it yet?"

"Think of what?" she asked, then grinned. "I was teasing you. No, I'm sorry. I've been trying, but I can't remember the name. It was right there, almost, first thing this morning, like I told you, but I couldn't quite make it pop through." She laughed and leaned closer to him. "Hey, that camper; I mean it was just great! Everything's so compact and handy. Maybe we can go on a trip after we get back from the Islands. Like a week's drive somewhere."

"Maybe. First, we remember that name. That's your job. Until you remember, I'm locking you in a closet in our hotel."

She let her eyes flare wide, brows lifted. "You do and I'll scream to everyone right now that you have a bomb planted in your crotch," she whispered. But she couldn't hold the angry pose and giggled. "I mean I should know about that bomb, shouldn't I, and how it certainly does go off with a bang!"

"Let's just concentrate on the name. Pretty soon they'll be serving something to eat or drink again. Now try. Close your eyes and relate to the time and the people, and relax; let the name come through."

"Hey, I bet you could hypnotize me."

"The name, Drisa. Close those pretty brown eyes and try."

Three hours later they circled Diamond Head and came in toward Honolulu's International Airport. Drisa still had not thought of the name. Her nose was pressed against the window and she gave a running commentary on the appearance of the island below.

"It's so green, and lots of buildings, and the water is a heavenly blue, and all those boats! Oh, Diamond Head! And the old fort, and the water!"

She had told him the name she was trying to think of was a strange one, more like part of it was a title.

They landed with a gentle bump and then they were at the unloading ramp. Drisa was disappointed when they came out of the ramp into the terminal and she saw that only members of tour groups were getting plumeria leis and kisses on the cheek. Mark bought two leis, draped them around her neck, and kissed her on the lips. He had wondered about her little-girl reactions, but decided this might be the real Drisa, rather than the sophisticate at the party.

"Welcome to Hawaii," he said; then they went to claim their luggage. Drisa watched everything. She saw the place where you could buy fresh pineapples and send them home. He had a hard time getting her past the florist shop.

Mark had been to Hawaii several times, and her childlike delight in everything new amused him. They found their luggage, picked up their reserved rental car, and began a slow drive along Nimitz Highway toward the Waikiki section of Honolulu, about ten miles away.

"Look, a banana tree with all these bananas on it. They're growing upside down!" Drisa shouted it, making Mark tense for a second at the wheel. She had doubled up her feet and sat on them on the seat so she could see better. Her glance went darting from one side of the road to the other, not wanting to miss a thing.

"It's so *green*, here. My God, think of the water bills they must have to pay." They rode in silence for a while.

"Look at that! Oh, Arnie, stop, stop please! What in the world is that strange thing?"

Mark pulled to the curb and looked where she pointed. It was a huge banyan tree with dozens of sturdy air root-secondary trunks.

"Is that one tree or a whole forest?" she asked.

"It's a banyan tree. You'll see lots of them here. They send down air roots that touch the ground, and grow into the dirt and keep on growing. The air roots turn into new trunks for the tree and sometimes get three or four feet thick. The air root trunks soon help hold up the tree. I've seen some of these banyan trees more than a hundred feet across at the top."

"One tree? You're kidding me."

"Wait until you see the one down in the International Market Place. Then you decide."

Drisa rolled down the window and stuck her head out. "It *smells* so good here! It really does, not at all like Los Angeles."

Mark drove again, into Kalakaua Avenue, which wound through the Waikiki area. He'd made reservations at the Princess Kaiulani Hotel. It wasn't the biggest or the fanciest one, but it was in Waikiki and just a block from the beach. It was also big enough so it was easy to get reservations. He remembered that all the signs in the hotel were written in both Japanese and English because the hotel is owned by Japanese and they cater to a heavy stream of Tokyo tour groups.

Mark drove along Kalakaua past the International Market Place on his left, then turned left into Kaiulani Avenue and, after half a block, swept into the circular hotel driveway. He left the car with a parking attendant and a bellboy brought their baggage as they checked in.

As Mark registered, Drisa walked around the lobby.

61

She came back and held onto his arm, whispering into his ear:

"You sure we want to stay here? The place is full of yang, you know, Orientals. Japanese all over the place!" Mark grinned and caught her hand as they followed the bellboy to their room at the fifth floor front. They would have a perfect view of the colorful King's Alley flea market right across the way.

After the bellboy left they stood on the little balcony hanging over the sidewalk and could see the edge of Waikiki Beach just a block away. Music floated up to them and Mark pointed down. In the front of King's Alley flea market a tall Hawaiian man stood with a microphone in hand singing Hawaiian songs. A Hawaiian guitar accompanied him. He finished a set of three songs and invited the forty or fifty people who had stopped to listen, to come up and buy one of his records.

"Hey, this is all just perfect!" Drisa said hugging him. "Do we have time to take a drive before it gets dark? I don't want to waste one precious second. Let's go on a long drive and see some of the island!"

He led her back inside and set her down at the small desk.

"First the name. We're here now, and I must have that name. If you don't remember it by tomorrow noon, I'm pushing you on board the next plane and it's back to the mainland for you."

"You wouldn't do that! I just got here. I haven't seen anything yet."

"And I don't like getting conned. Either you come up with that name or get ready to end your free vacation."

Mark gave her a pen and paper at the desk and picked up the telephone book. He sat down on the bed

62

and opened it to the H's. There was no Hawaiian Multimedia, Inc., or any name that even came close, listed in the book. He called the airport and asked for the air freight office. They told him there was no material in will call for Hawaiian Multimedia. Yes, the clerk remembered handling some other material for them, but nothing was waiting now.

Mark put down the phone and eyed the pretty girl. "You, small girl, sit in that chair and think. I have to go to the newspaper office and check some files. Be sure you have that name for me when I get back."

The Honolulu *Star-Bulletin* had a good morgue. They called it a library, and a woman in her sixties of mixed Oriental ancestry showed Mark the file on pornographic stories. There were three or four dozen in the past four years. Mark went through them and found only two that had any tie to pedophiles at all. Both involved small photo studios and the taking of lewd photos. The men arrested were fined only, not jailed. The items were dated a little over two years ago. Mark wrote down the addresses and names of the firms and later checked the phone books. Neither studio was in business now, or at least didn't have a telephone.

It was a little after 3:00 when he got back to the hotel. Drisa had filled up two sheets scribbling and writing down names. She evidently had really been trying. She showed him the pages and shook her head.

Mark peeled off a hundred-dollar bill from his pocket money clip. "Here, go buy yourself a muumuu and some puka shell necklaces. Have some fun. It might relax you enough so you'll think of it. I have some more work to do."

She jumped up and kissed him, holding him so tightly he thought she might never let go.

"Oh, you're a darling, after all! For a while there, I

was worried. But now I'll relax and I *will* remember. I can almost promise you that. When should I be back?"

He looked at his watch, which he had set to Hawaiian time. "By 7:00, and we'll have a mini luau somewhere. Now scoot."

She jumped forward and kissed him again, then hurried out the door. She had changed clothes while he had been gone, and now wore a revealing blue halter top, short shorts, and sandals. He shrugged, after all, this was Hawaii.

As soon as she left, Mark went to the lobby, found an empty phone booth, and closed the door. He called the first number on the pedophile league list he had taken from the Valley. It had a Honolulu number, so he dialed and waited. Someone picked it up on the fifth ring.

"Yeah?" a woman asked.

"Hello. I'm a stranger in town and I had your number to call to talk about our mutual work in the league. I hope you can help me."

"Listen, buster. That's an old list. We're not into that sort of thing, anymore. You tell them to get our name off that list! You don't and I'm changing my number. Now don't you dare call again, just leave us alone! We're straight now, so, Goddamnit, you leave us the hell alone!" She slammed down the phone.

Mark lifted his brows at the anger in the voice. He could understand it. He looked at the only other Hawaiian number listed. It was on Kauai. The Penetrator got out a handful of quarters and asked how much it was to call the Garden Island. The phone rang just twice before someone answered.

"Good afternoon." It was a slow, easy woman's voice.

"Hello, I'm from the mainland and I have your num-

64

ber to call about our mutual league friends. We're in the same league and this is the contact number to help out strangers, right?"

"Could be."

"Well, I'm here for only a few days and the contact here in Honolulu evidently is out of business. So, I'm looking."

"If you're really who you say, you should know the number there has not been functional for six months. I think you should check in through the Tipped Canoe Club on Seaside Avenue. If you're a paid-up member, they'll be able to help you. Now, don't bother me again."

Mark hung up and studied the pocket map of Waikiki. He found Seaside Avenue only five or six blocks away, so he decided to walk.

Honolulu hadn't changed much since he'd been there before. The big new hotel across from the Princess Kaiulani had been finished. Other new buildings were climbing into the sky. The population still seemed to be growing more Oriental by the day. The last time he knew there was no majority ethnic group in Hawaii. No one racial stock had more than fifty percent of the population. Rather it was a state of five or six major minorities, including Caucasians.

The Tipped Canoe turned out to be a bar with a little restaurant, but not many people were eating. There was a small dance floor and a place for a combo, lots of tables and two bars. The place was jumping already, and disco music flowed from records; a spinning mirror ball on the ceiling shot out a million stabs of reflected light sprinkling the whole club with its impulses.

Mark slid onto a stool at one end of the bar and ordered a beer. The barkeep who served him was Chinese, Mark thought, or perhaps Tahitian and Japanese with a little Hawaiian. He gave up trying to guess the man's heritage. When he came by the next time Mark signaled.

Mark spoke slowly and softly. "They told me I could get some help here. We're in the same league, and I'm just in town from the mainland. Some guy in Kauai said I should check in here."

The man frowned. "No understand," he said and left.

Mark waited for him to come back past and reached out.

"Hey, you. I'm getting impatient. This is a checkout spot for the league. Fine, I'm checking. I want some action and don't waste the whole Goddamned night. You hear me?"

The Oriental's eyes seemed to turn into angry slits. He sighed and waved to the rear. "Okay, okay. No trouble."

From the far end of the bar two of the biggest Chinese men Mark had ever seen walked toward him. Both were over six-feet-six and three hundred pounds. One of them motioned for Mark to follow him and then walked ahead. The other man fell in step behind Mark. They went through a beaded curtain, then into a store-room, and the next thing Mark knew he had been shoved by the man behind him and sent skidding through a back door and into the alley behind the club.

The men said something in Chinese to him, laughed, then closed the door, and Mark heard a metal bolt slam into place. At least they had noticed him, and the word *league* had caused a minor stir. Now he'd go back in and try again, this time with more persuasion.

Mark dusted himself off and went down the alley to the street and back to the front door. This time he had his hand in his jacket and his .45 in his hand. When he

66

got to the end of the bar he motioned the barkeep over, grabbed him by his shirtfront and dragged him around the counter and past the beaded curtain; then he jammed the .45 under the Chinaman's chin and pushed the barrel upward into the soft flesh.

"Now, Charlie Chan, I want some answers. Either I get them fast or you meet your favorite ancestors from the Ming Dynasty. Do I make myself clear?"

The man nodded, eyes wild. He called out something in Chinese and almost at once the two large men appeared, saw the .45, and backed away. A small Chinese man, in Oriental robes and a black cap appeared from another door, and bowed to Mark.

"I came here for some simple answers and these two meat-axes threw me into the alley. Do I have to punch holes in a few people to get some information? What the hell is wrong with you fuckers anyway?"

The small man came forward, nodded again, and now Mark didn't know if he were Chinese or Japanese. "Sorry to misunderstand you, sir. My cousin at the bar is here from Hong Kong only two weeks and is not good yet with the English. Small mistake. You are man with the league, correct? No problem. I have phone number on card. Just say Tom Kim told you call. They will help."

"The number's here in town?"

"Yes, indeed."

Mark lowered the .45 from the man's throat and pushed him away.

"Just take care of this guy. I don't like his attitude."

Mark walked back through the beaded curtain and saw three large black men come into the club. They were the first blacks Mark had seen since landing at the airport. Blacks are not a large part of the Hawaiian

67

population. All three were well dressed and seemed to be known there. A small Chinese waitress bowed them to a corner booth. They sat, and the girl quickly brought a round of drinks without the usual ordering. Either the men had preordered or were regular customers.

Mark left by the front door this time, the .45 safely tucked away in his clip-on holster, as he wondered who the three black men were. A rock group? Maybe. Or baseball players with the Honolulu Islanders team in the triple A league? Mark gave up on it, looked again at the phone number penciled on the card, and walked toward a telephone booth a block down the street.

CHAPTER 6

Your Basic Mattress Ploy

It was 6:15 as Mark sat in the phone booth. He waited five minutes and didn't see anyone come out of the Tipped Canoe Club who seemed to be following him. No Chinese appeared or anyone who looked otherwise suspicious. Mark dialed the number the Chinese had given him, but got only a busy signal. He left the booth and walked down Seaside to Kuhio Avenue, past the Coral Reef Hotel, then past the Kuhio Hotel and the Outrigger East, before he turned right toward his own hotel on Kaiulani. In the lobby he dialed the number again from a booth in the far corner. It rang.

"Good evening and aloha," a pleasant woman's voice answered.

"Well, aloha to you. That's a nice greeting. Hey, I'm new in the Islands and I lost your number. Good old Tom Kim reminded me of it. He says that you and I are in the same league."

"Well, good. A double aloha and a double welcome

to you. I bet you're interested in some league-type entertainment."

"That certainly would be nice. Any suggestions?"

"Plenty. Your first name, please?"

"Oh, yeah. I'm Arnie."

"Well, Arnie, we're absolutely filled up for tonight, but if you give me a call tomorrow and tell me your first name again, I'll have some definite action reserved for you and give you the time and place and style."

"Nothing for tonight?"

"I'm sorry, Arnie. This is our busy season."

"Oh, yeah, I should have thought of that. Well, I'm here on business, so I'll get that done, and then be ready."

"You do that, Arnie. I'm sure you'll be pleased with our service. I'll hear from you tomorrow. Aloha."

"Aloha means good-bye too? What a crazzzzzzzzzzzzzy place."

A few minutes later, upstairs in their room, he found Drisa trying on some new clothes. She had found a little shop six blocks over.

"It had these fantastic muumuus for only twelve dollars! Can you imagine? I'd pay forty dollars for this one in Los Angeles, and the same one would be eighty-five in Beverly Hills. It was so cheap I bought a matching aloha shirt for you, Arnie."

She got it and made him put it on. Mark did so and then glanced at the pad of paper on the desk. The only thing on it were the initials "P.M." He looked at her. She came and stood close to him, leaning in.

"Sorry, that's all I've been able to come up with, but I'm getting there. Those initials, P.M., are the same ones we saw in the studio back in LA. Remember? The initials on that letter. Right now I'm stuck with Paul Muni and Paul McCartney."

"That's not much return for a free trip to Hawaii."

"You mean I've got to earn my passage?"

"Of course. You think this is charity?"

She pulled off her muumuu, showing her naked, jiggling breasts with nipples starting to surge with excitement. Below she wore only pale-blue panties.

"I could make a quick payment on my debt right now."

"You're tempting me, Drisa," Mark said with a firm smile. "But right now I'd rather you kept your mind on your work. A half-hour at the desk with the pencil. Then we go for dinner." She shrugged and floated the red hibiscus-flowered-print muumuu back over her head. Then she pouted. But she took up the pen and sat at the desk doodling.

Mark went through the *Star-Bulletin* newspaper he had brought up from the lobby, but found nothing touching his project. The half-hour wasn't quite up when he finished the paper, but he motioned to Drisa.

"Come on, let's go for some food. I promised you a luau, so let's see what we can find."

Drisa bounced from the chair, laughing. She was a frisky fourteen again, her pout gone, a smile on her pretty face, and she grabbed him with a hug.

"Oh, wow! This is exciting. I don't know when I've had so much fun! What about Don Ho? Can we go see him? Doesn't he work at one of the big clubs here? Wouldn't they have a dinner show or a luau or something?"

Mark said they would ask at the desk, and went downstairs.

Two hours later they were in the middle of the most food Mark could ever remember seeing. The Princess Kaiulani Hotel had a luau of its own and Mark was just in time to get reservations for the 8:00 P.M. start. That meant they had almost an hour, so they walked around the corner to the International Market Place. Mark showed Drisa the huge banyan tree in the middle of the area filled with stores and shops and restaurants. He proved to her that the air roots in reality did become large new trunks to help hold up the giant of a tree. These air roots came down twenty, thirty, sometimes forty feet away from the main trunk.

"I still don't believe that's just one tree," Drisa said. He bought her some shell jewelry and then one piece of jade, since she said she didn't have any. It was a ring with a round stone.

She kissed him and then sang as they walked back to the hotel.

At the luau Mark passed on the poi and the raw fish, had seconds on the mahi mahi, and concentrated on the pineapple and pork. He would feel fat and full for a week, but right then it didn't matter. The long tables were so loaded with food Mark found it impossible to believe there were enough people to eat all of it.

The time was nearly 11:00 when the food was gone, and the traditional Hawaiian dances performed and the spectacle over. They walked around a block or two to settle their meal.

"It's so warm outside," Drisa said, her eyes sparkling. "Here it is 11:00 at night and it's seventy, maybe seventy-five, degrees. It's beautiful!" She held both arms in the air and twirled around. "Oh, God, but I could learn to like it here. The weather is just marvelous, and all that yummy food!"

He caught her hand and angled her back toward the hotel.

"I'm glad you liked the show. Now you should be all relaxed and ready to work. We're going into a one-hundred percent think-tank operation. I'll help. We'll go through every man's name starting with *P* we can think of if you want."

"Oh, we have to?" she asked, whining.

"Yes. That's why you're here, remember?"

In the room a few minutes later, she pulled the drapes, cutting out the soft Hawaiian night air, and then peeled out of her muumuu. She stood there wearing only the soft-blue panties.

"Oh, I hope you don't mind. I just love to go topless. I get a wild sense of freedom. And it seems more friendly."

He took her hand, led her to the desk, and eased her into the chair.

"Topless, bottomless, I don't care. Just remember the name."

She scowled, shrugged, and bent over the paper.

Mark let her worry and wiggle and sigh for a half-hour before he pulled the other chair up beside her.

"Any progress?"

"I don't know. At first I thought I had it. Manny seemed so right for a while. But then it didn't seem right."

Mark put the name into his computerlike memory but came up with nothing. He wasn't the one who was supposed to remember the name, let alone recognize it.

"Manny, as the first name or last? P. M. would make it the last."

"That doesn't seem right," she said, and stood, pacing back and forth in the room.

Mark watched her and he was sure she accented each little wiggle, each sway of her breasts. She was really trying to get him all sexed up so she could quit the memory game and play another one.

She scowled, but the expression faded into a grin.

"Hey, I've got it. His last name was Mann. Not Manny, just Mann, with two *n*'s! That much I remember, but now all we need is a first name. All of them seem wrong. Fred Mann, Harry Mann, Horace Mann. That one is familiar, but that was the name of my junior high."

Mark watched her, not wanting to interfere with the process, with the word relationship. Hoping that it all would come together. He did not react to the last name. There were millions of people in the world with that last name.

Mark sat on the bed now and watched her. She seemed to be trying to get the first name, really concentrating.

"You said we'd go through the men's names starting with *P*; name me some," she said.

"Okay. Pablo, Paco, Paul, Phillip, Paddy, Patrick, Pierre, even Pancho and Peter. Any help?"

She made a strange face. "Nope. I don't think it's a real name. I mean like I said before, more of a title."

"A title? Like doctor, senator, mayor, or chef?" Mark asked.

"Yeah, something like that." Then she jumped up and shouted. "Hey! I've got it. Damned if I didn't remember it! His name is *Preacher Mann*. Preacher is that title."

Mark stood now too, amazement, disbelief on his face. He caught her shoulders and turned her to face him. "Are you sure? Are you absolutely sure that is his name?"

"Damned right. Look, I said it was. I just spent two days racking my little pea brain trying to figure out what the Goddamned name was and that's it."

A thousand memories shot back at Mark. He sat down on the bed. Preacher Mann, the amazingly evil black man he had battled in Florida waters a few years back when the big man was trying to perfect a method of freezing beautiful girls and thawing them out when he needed them for an international call-girl operation.

The big man had operated on the Florida mainland and on his own private island seven miles off the coast. He had built an impregnable fortress, with most of it underwater, where he had dozens of cryogenic cells and frozen animals, and where he experimented with human beings, freezing them and trying to bring them back to life again as they thawed.

Mark never knew for sure if the big man had escaped the final explosion and destruction of the island laboratory, but evidently he had.

Preacher Mann!

The more Mark thought about the Preacher, the more he realized that he should have seen the indelible stamp of that criminal genius. Preacher had simply found another form of sexual misconduct to take advantage of, to grow rich on, and with it to exploit hundreds of innocent children in the process.

"Hey, you go deaf, Arnie? I been trying to talk to you."

Mark looked up, and saw the girl in front of him.

"You heard about this guy before or something?"

"Heard of him?" Mark nodded. "Oh, yes, I've heard of him."

"And you think he's the one behind this international league thing and the kiddy sex? I saw that envelope in your stuff and read part of it. You really going after that guy?"

"Yes. This Preacher Mann, is he black?"

"True, a big one. Hell, he must be six-three and weighs a ton!"

"That's the one."

75

Drisa began pulling down her blue panties. "Hey, now that I remembered the name, you interested in messing around a little? I mean don't I get some kind of a reward?"

"Drisa, you do, but right now I've got work to do."

"Now? It's almost 11:30, midnight."

"The phone book won't care." Mark pulled out the Honolulu directory. Under the *M*'s there was half a column of listings in the name of Mann. There was no one with an initial *P* or Preacher as the first name. It figured.

When Mark looked up he saw that Drisa had put on her muumuu and sandals.

"You nuts or something, Arnie? I mean what's all this jazz about trying to get even with somebody you hardly know. What's he done to you, anyway?"

"Drisa, you don't understand. Do you think it's right to take young children and inflict a sex act on them and take pictures of it so some mentally disturbed people can have pleasure from it? Is that normal behavior to you?"

"Well, hell. I guess not. But that's what we got cops for. Let the cops do all that. I want to have fun in Hawaii!"

"So have fun. I'm going to work."

She pulled out her bags, which she really hadn't unpacked, and dumped the rest of her clothes and toilet articles into them.

"I'm leaving."

"Fine. What will you use for money?"

"You'll give me some."

"Nope."

"Then I'll work the streets."

She put her two suitcases in the hall; then picked up her purse and pulled out a .32 automatic. "I'm leaving;

you're staying here. They thought you might be the same one. They said if you recognized the name Preacher Mann, you were the Penetrator. So this is how it had to be right from the first." Her face was hard now, gone was the playacting youthful excitement.

She didn't draw it out or try to be fancy. Drisa simply started shooting.

Mark had that split-second trigger-finger warning and dove behind the bed to the far wall. He felt one slug whistle past his ear, and another one nicked his pants leg. Then he was below the bed top, grabbing the mattress and lifting it, tipping it upward toward the girl. He shoved the mattress, heard it absorb two more rounds; then the top tipped downward and crashed to the floor well off the bed.

The Penetrator darted around it, but the girl wasn't under the mattress or sprawled beyond it. The door was open.

As he had tipped the mattress she must have been scampering for the door. He ran to it and stepped into the hallway. Twenty-five middle-aged Japanese men and women stood there on both sides of his door, their suitcases in the hall, and all were quietly arguing among themselves. He couldn't see Drisa.

A young Japanese man who must have been the tour guide came up and apologized.

"Sorry, sir. I seems we are on the wrong floor after all. I tried to tell the young lady who just left with her bags we weren't trying to break into her room."

Mark waved and looked around. Her bags were gone. With the crush in the hallway and her lead he would never catch her now. Mark walked back to his room, his face crinkled into a frown.

"They said . . . They thought . . ." The girl had used both phrases. The Preacher had almost won. Drisa had been a plant from the first, and he had been taken in. He should have played his hunch that night in Beverly Hills and left her there. Now it would be just that much harder. His calculated risk had almost backfired. At least now he knew who he was facing.

CHAPTER 7

Three for the Show

Mark Hardin stood in the hallway for a few seconds watching the confused jumble of Japanese tourists picking up bags and wandering toward the elevator.

He would have to leave the hotel. Drisa knew who he was and where he was staying. So he had to check out as soon as possible.

Five minutes later Mark had finished packing and was at the front desk. One item on his bill he noted with interest: Drisa had made four phone calls while she was there and the switchboard bill showed the numbers contacted.

A half-hour later Mark had checked into a less-expensive and more out-of-the way hotel, the White Sands. He had driven around in his rental car for ten minutes before he settled on it. By that time he was certain no car was following him. Not even a three-car switch could have fooled him.

As soon as the Penetrator dropped his suitcases on the bed, he looked at the phone numbers on his hotel bill. Two of them he recognized: Tom Kim's and the league contact. He dialed the third one but there was no answer. The fourth number was a drugstore and it answered even though it was after midnight.

Mark lay on the bed, his fingers laced together behind his head. What other angles did he have? The league connection phone was the best one, but that would wait for morning. A second might be the *Life Child* distributors. First the retailers, then to the wholesaler. If he could find the magazines locally he might work back to the distributor, then to the source.

Yes, it was a good plan.

The Penetrator took a quick shower and went to bed with his mental alarm clock set for 6:30. It should be an interesting day.

By 8:00 the next morning Mark had found the porno shops. They were well away from the tourists on the Waikiki strand. The little street had no sign. Only half a signpost remained where an errant car had smashed it down. Four porno shops nestled in a row, and in the windows of each was a display of *Life Child,* with the cover pictures half shielded with a bumper sticker promoting a hotel. He tried the door. Locked. A sign said it would be open from 11:00 A.M. to 11:00 P.M. Mark had a firm plan worked out now. Since he had no direct lead to the supplier, he would let the supplier find him. Easy.

First, he'd make a call to the league contact, and see how strongly it was set up. He had only a phone number not an address, but it wouldn't be too hard. Mark found a phone book and dialed.

"Aloha and good morning. May I help you?"

"Hi there, this is the telephone repairman. I got a bum address on your service-work call. The dispatcher must have messed up and read the wrong address. Now, I could call back and tell him he's crazy, but he don't like me too damn much anyway, know what I mean?"

"Right. Oh yes. I've got a boss myself."

"Right. So, instead of getting all messed up with my boss, why don't you just give me your right address and I'll be there before the sun goes down."

"I didn't know we had a trouble call in."

"Oh, hell, not a trouble call. It's a service update on some of your equipment. Found a defective part in some of your handsets that could short out and cause burns."

"Well, we don't want that to happen, do we?"

She gave him the address; he wrote it down, thanked her, and went to his rented Pinto. Mark looked at his map. The address was just off Kalanianaole Highway out beyond Diamond Head and just past Koko Head. The street number was 284 Kiko.

Mark drove past the place twice before he was sure he had the right spot. It was a private residence, had three older cars parked in front and one in the driveway. A jumble of telephone lines went into the garage, and Mark decided they had told the neighbors they had a small telephone-answering service.

Mark had worn his new aloha shirt that morning and now knocked on the front door and waited. It took several minutes before anyone came. Then the panel opened cautiously and a woman's face with hair curlers around it peered through the crack.

"Building inspector," Mark said firmly, and with authority. "We have a report that you're conducting an illegal business operation in a residential area. I'll have to inspect the premises."

"Oh, no. That was the old answering service. That went broke six months ago." The woman said it with sadness.

81

"Then show me where the operation was conducted so I can finish my report," Mark countered.

"I can't do that. My husband isn't home."

Mark pushed firmly on the door, shoving it open, and was moving the woman back. He stepped inside. "I'm afraid I'll have to insist on seeing it."

"Hey, you can't break in here!" the woman shouted. She was small, and at least part Hawaiian. Mark walked along a short hall to the kitchen, with the woman right behind him. He saw another door that should lead into the garage. When he opened it he found himself in a converted area that was now a family room and office. One side held three business desks, each with two telephones on it, and each with a young woman at the desk. Two of them were busy on the phones. The older woman ran behind him screeching. The girls looked around, curious.

"The International League doesn't like the way you're running their operation here. We are severing your connection." Mark went to the first desk and jerked a telephone set, snapping the wires from the wall connection. He pulled out the other five phones and put them carefully down on the desk. Then he picked up clipboards that had schedules on them, tore off the first page on the three boards, and put the pages in his pocket.

Mark took a small thermite bomb from his other pocket. It was a new type, and guaranteed to burn with a searing heat for four minutes. There was absolutely no way to put it out, since it generated its own oxygen supply as it burned.

The women huddled in one corner, not knowing what to do.

"Ladies, I'd suggest you pick up your gear and get out of here. This place is going to be too hot to handle in about five minutes. There will be cops and firemen all over the place." Mark put some cardboard cartons and paper at one side against the drapes over the window. He piled a wooden chair on it, then an overstuffed chair, put the thermite device below the whole thing and ignited it. Almost at once the flames spread to the cardboard, up the drapes to the ceiling. The wood began to burn, then the chair, and a moment later the window glass popped outward.

Two of the women ran into the kitchen. Mark followed the last two and, as he came through the door, the older Hawaiian woman lunged at him with a butcher knife. Mark sidestepped, slammed the side of his right hand down hard on the woman's forearm, breaking both bones and jolting the knife to the floor.

"Don't ever play with sharp toys, lady, you could get hurt." Then he walked out the front door and to his car. As he drove away he saw smoke coming from the broken window, and several neighbors were on their lawns looking. He was sure the fire department and police would be arriving soon. The league connection with the Hawaiian world on this island was at least crippled for a few days. Tom Kim would have another one set up soon, probably within a week.

Mark drove along the beautiful Kalanianaole Highway toward Diamond Head, turned off toward Kahala on Kalakaua Avenue and wound his way into Waikiki. He found the porn shops again and parked half a block away, then walked back.

All he had to do was draw enough attention to himself and he was sure it wouldn't take long for someone to find him. And that should lead right on up the ladder to the top . . . to Preacher Mann. Amazing how that man kept bobbing up in one racket after another.

HAWAIIAN ADULT BOOKS, the first store's sign

said. It was a small shop about the size of a living room, but jammed full of adult books and magazines. In back he found a stack of *Life Child* magazines. Mark stood there and began tearing them in half. He opened the sixty-page magazine and tore it along the staples. Mark had ripped six of them in half when someone ran toward him.

"What the hell are you doing?" the man asked. He was small, with glasses, a necktie, and a sweater vest.

"What the hell does it look like?" Mark asked, tore in half another *Life Child* magazine, and threw it at the man.

"Those are worth fifteen dollars each, and I'm going to charge you for each one you've ruined."

"Fine with me, you go right ahead and charge me for them, because I'd rather owe you than pay up." Mark tore another in half. There were only two more on the stack. He grabbed one and ripped it as another man walked up. This one was bigger, about six-feet and two hundred pounds.

"What's the matter, Harry?" he asked, then looked at the torn magazines. "Oh, oh. We've got a purist."

The man swung a roundhouse right that he telegraphed all the way from New Jersey. Mark half blocked it, caught the fist, and jerked the big man forward and slammed him into a standing wire rack of books. The man crashed through it and brought the whole thing down on top of him.

"Nice to make your acquaintance," Mark said. Then he tore the last magazine in half, gave it to Harry, the proprietor, and walked out the front door.

He did the same thing in the next shop, LAVA ADULT BOOKS, but they had only six *Life Child* left.

The manager just threw up his hands and shook his head.

In the third shop they were ready for Mark, and tried to lock the front door. Mark kicked it in and grinned.

"Hey, nice of you chaps to meet me at the door. Where do you keep your stack of *Life Child* magazines? Never mind, I'll find them."

The man in charge was young, maybe twenty-two.

"Don't touch my stock or I'll call the police," the man said.

Mark grinned. "Yeah, you just do that, and I'll swear how you sell this shit to the kids under eighteen, and how you deal on the side in pot and coke. You go right ahead and call the boys in blue, in fact I'll even dial the number for you."

The manager scowled and closed his eyes for a moment. Then he turned, and Mark found the display of *Life Child*, twelve copies. He ripped them in half, and left the shop.

It was almost the same scene at the fourth store. He did his work, wondering when someone was going to meet him with some muscle, or at least some authority. How long did it take to get word to the bosses in this outfit? He tore the last book in half and tossed it to the manager, a woman who just shrugged as he went out the door.

When he came from the shop he saw a pickup truck slide to a stop at the curb. Three big black men, all over six-feet tall, and all wearing fancy clothes, jumped out of the pickup and had a short conference as they looked at him. Then they grinned.

That's when Mark remembered them. They were the

same three dudes he had seen at Tom Kim's place, the Tipped Canoe.

"Hey, man," one of them called. "You the honkie who likes to tear up magazines? Ya, you the one. We got some business with you."

Then all three lifted baseball bats out of the pickup and held them high as they charged at Mark.

CHAPTER 8

Preacher Mann's Playpen

This was the best time of any day, Preacher Mann decided as he slid behind the table and looked over a tray that his private chef had just brought in. After years of a vegetarian diet, Preacher had expanded his scope to include seafood. This was one of his six meals a day, nothing heavy, not a lot of food at any one time, but a continuous supply of fuel to energize his big frame.

His real name was Peter Doxford Mann, he was thirty-eight years old, Negroid, six-feet four-inches tall, and weighed in at two hundred and sixty-eight pounds. With all his size he was still a superbly conditioned man, swam every day, went skin diving when he could, and worked out in the weight room and on the punching bag every day.

His gleaming black head was totally bald and he kept it that way with a close shave every morning. The skinhead accented his large jug-handled ears and oversized brown eyes. Preacher's nose had flaring nostrils over thick lips.

He finished eating the snails and asked the chef how he had prepared them.

"Ah, yes. First I sauté the snails in Burgundy wine, then stuff them in the shell with a secret mixture of the snails, garlic-splashed parsley and butter."

Preacher nodded. For his entrée he had ordered shrimp, and they came, jumbos tempura-style, served on a sea of lettuce. For his drink he had a chilled combination of juice of the papaya, pineapple, and guava. When he was satisfied, Preacher waved away the food tray and sat on a Japanese floor bed, then stretched out for a fifteen-minute nap.

The room was Japanese style, with tatami mats on the floor, delicate Japanese watercolor paintings in the alcoves along the wall, and a brilliantly painted folding screen blocking out the windows. Classical kabuki dance music played softly over four speakers placed precisely in the room to give the discordant Oriental music the greatest possible mellowness.

Exactly fifteen minutes after he lay down, Preacher sat up on the bed and waved. A low Japanese table carried by two black men was brought into the room and placed in front of the huge one, then another man came in and sat across from Preacher. The new man was Kim Soong, a Korean with one eye, and the best business administrator Preacher had ever worked with. Kim treated him as an equal, knowing that together they had built up the business and spread it across three continents.

"Disquieting news, Mr. Mann. We have heard from Drisana. She has at last admitted to knowing your name, which costs us nothing. When she told him, the man gave himself away, and now we know for sure that he is the *Penetrator*, and that he is here looking for you and your operation. There can be no doubt now. The reports from the mainland were true. Drisana tried to kill him as you ordered, but she missed. She said he simply dodged the bullets, dove behind the bed, and threw the whole mattress at her. She said she was lucky to get away."

"So, the Penetrator comes for me again," Preacher said, grimly. "This time it will be his last. We shall not make the same mistakes we did before. Now we know our enemy."

He nodded, remembering. "Our first mission is to kill the troublemaker. We will not attempt an honorable kill, or try to be sporting, Mr. Soong. With the Penetrator you kill him any way you can, anytime, in anyplace. Shoot him in the back if you can while his hands and feet are tied and he is blindfolded. Then throw him under a diesel truck and dump his remains in a cement mixer. Then he *may* be dead. You get him any way you can."

Preacher looked at Soong. "I know this isn't your field of expertise, but remember that this man is an expert at all types of combat, jungle fighting and hand-to-hand warfare. He stayed alive in Vietnam for two or three years, the newspapers said. He's blown more men away than he can count. He was shooting the eyes out of Viet Cong headmen and generals when you were learning to use your goddamn abacus."

"Sir, we have assigned four double-hit teams to track him down. We missed him at his former hotel because he left almost at once after the girl did, so we had no chance there. I have our best men on the job. They will not fail, do not worry."

"I always worry, you little Korean bastard. That's why both of us are still alive." He paused and smiled at the small man. There was a symbiotic relationship between them that the Preacher had never understood, not even after three years. They were complete opposites; yet they functioned together brilliantly.

"Mr. Soong, you have made your periodic check on our circle of defense?"

"Indeed, Mr. Mann. We have our own people in every house in the encircling compound. We now have filled in the voids in our line and have all twenty houses in the circle around the three sides of the mansion that are inhabited. It's a wall of steel; no one can get through. The steel mesh fence behind those houses is now all in place, creating an ideal guard and buffer zone. And of course we have a homeowners' association which has put up the guard post and gate at the entrance to the only access road into the circle drive and to the mansion."

"We're probably going to need it all, Mr. Soong. The Penetrator is a devil, as hard to catch and kill as a breath of wind. But this time we will get him. We have the advantage. He's on our turf, and he's running around blind."

A messenger came in and gave Mr. Soong a sheet of paper, then backed out the door.

Soong read it quickly, then looked up at the black man.

"You may be right, Mr. Mann. It seems that your Penetrator friend, or someone equally as adept, has just torn up, and burned down the International League's new clientele's contact near Koko Head. Firemen were there to put out the fire, and the police were asking a lot of questions."

"The serpent strikes quickly. I hope your D-squads are alert and watchful, Mr. Soong." Preacher was silent a moment. Mr. Soong sat across from him, his legs folded, waiting.

"Mr. Soong, I believe you had a surprise for me, a tour of the latest in our security precautions."

"Correct. It is ready."

They walked to an elevator concealed in the far end of the thirty-foot-long room, and descended three flights to the ground level. Outside the elevator they both put on Japanese-style sandals with the strap between the toes, and walked upward along a crushed seashell path, some fifty feet from the building.

Preacher Mann stopped and looked back.

"It was a good move of yours, Mr. Soong, to buy this Japanese mansion and expand it. The construction work gave us plenty of chance to do the additional work we had to do in the other areas."

The traditional Japanese house seemed to blend with the surrounding garden so well that at first the building appeared modest. But as the eye followed its lines the viewer saw a magnificent three-story, princely mansion, built entirely in the Japanese style, with sliding partitions, lots of exposed natural wood, rice-paper panels. Inside there were tatami mats on the floor and much highly varnished woodwork. The gardens surrounding the back of the mansion were both delicate and traditional, but at the same time functional, allowing a few broad paths for use when needed. Others ended abruptly in pools where one could see carp and multicolored five- and six-pound goldfish swimming peacefully.

Mr. Soong stopped at the largest pool, the one that extended along half the back of the mansion, built so it flowed under open balconies just over the water.

"And here, Mr. Mann, we have your prize. They came in by freighter in special tanks and only now are reviving enough to be at their best." Mr. Soong threw four slices of bread into the pool and the surface churned with a feeding frenzy. When the food was gone, calm returned to the surface.

"Amazing," Preacher said. "And they come only from South America, you say. Amazing."

They walked around the back of the estate where the gardens ended and the hillside took over in rocky and growth-covered ledges and bluffs.

"We have the new electronic fence back here, Mr. Mann. Automatically it transmits the position of anyone who tries to trespass. These are both sound-and-vibration-type sensors, and we get an instant readout in the security office.

At the front of the estate were more gardens, which extended down to the backyards of the private homes, and the eight-foot-high chain link fence. A narrow white seashell lane wound up from the street and the guard at the gate.

"We decided that the fence could not be electrified as you had requested, Mr. Mann. Several reasons, the biggest being the danger of an accident by an innocent child and the resulting horrible publicity and eventual government orders to turn off the juice. However, this should work very well. It also has the vibration sensors, and they are amplified by the very nature of the fencing."

The big man was getting tired of the tour. He led the way back to the mansion, and they sat in the Western-style reception room on the first floor.

As they talked another man brought Mr. Soong a written report. He studied it quickly, then smiled.

"Ah, Mr. Mann, a stroke of luck. We have had reports of a large man with a dark complexion tearing up copies of *Life Child* in bookstores. A persuasion squad of three men has been dispatched to meet the man as he comes from the next store."

"Not a persuasion squad, you fool!" Preacher bellowed. "It's probably the Penetrator trying to draw attention to himself so you'll send some men and he can grab one and question him until he cracks. Call them back, and send in your hit squads, all of them!"

Mr. Soong nodded, walked swiftly to a house phone, and spoke rapidly. When he returned to the couch, Preacher Mann had already got up.

"I'm going for a nap. Send up my two small friends, the Japanese today, I think." He watched Soong a moment for a reaction, found none, and walked away.

Kim Soong watched the big man leave and made one more phone call. He hoped that the hit squads got there in time to eliminate this latest challenge to their empire. Another two or three years and they both could quit with a hundred million each! He walked to the balcony over the water and watched the hungry fish swimming around in the big pool.

He had known little about Preacher Mann before he met him three years ago. Kim Soong had something of a reputation in the Islands as a man who could get things done that were semilegal or downright illegal. Mann interested Soong and he had a complete background investigation prepared on the man in New York and Miami.

He found that Preacher Mann began running numbers in Harlem when he was twelve, and by the time he was fifteen and in high school he turned his girl friend into a willing young whore and sold her to the other boys for two dollars a hump. By the time he was expelled from high school, he had three professional hookers, two blacks and a white. Three years later he was into pot and heroin. His pushing business grew until he was a supplier and then a distributor, and he owned half of the Harlem heroin trade. Then things began to go downhill and he got too hot for the big city, so he pulled out for Miami.

In New York he had gone back to night school when he was eighteen, got his diploma, and then signed on at CCNY. Eventually he won his Bachelor of Arts degree in Eastern European art. He saw no reason why a racketeer had to be a dumbbell.

In Miami he went semilegitimate, used his heroin earnings to buy a big office building, and owned controlling interests in a dozen other legitimate businesses. One was a coastwide shipping firm through which he ran tons of pot as well as disguised shipments of horse, coke, and hash.

He picked up his Preacher nickname in Miami when he turned vegetarian and went wild over the natural foods. He kept preaching about the glories of vegetarian eating; people began calling him the Preacher, and the name stuck.

The more his influence grew in southern Florida, the more he used it to get politicians under his wing. After ten years there he was virtually untouchable by the law. He didn't flaunt it, but if one of his men was picked up, he was bailed out quickly and quietly, the case usually becoming lost in the court's tremendous backlog of cases.

Preacher's crowning achievement in Florida had been his cryogenic island where he dreamed of selecting the most perfect girls in the world, freezing them, and thawing them out when he needed them for his growing international call-girl trade. Unfortunately, that was when the Penetrator moved into the picture and punctured the plans, the island, and the cryogenic sealed units, with resulting tremendous explosions that tore the island into nothing but a sunken reef.

Preacher Mann took care of his body. He didn't smoke, drink, or use drugs, but he had one weakness. Girls. Kim Soong knew what to expect upstairs. He was glad he didn't have to participate.

On the third floor, Preacher Mann stood looking out an open panel at the fishpond below. At one time he thought of putting the swimming pool there so he could dive in from the window. Now he was glad he hadn't.

A knock came at the panel, and he invited his visitors in.

Two solemn, pretty Japanese girls came in and stood just past the closed panel. Both were fifteen, had long sleekly black hair and bright black eyes.

"Come, come, pretty ones, don't be afraid. You've been here before, remember?"

The girls giggled, and slipped out of the long white robes they had worn. There was nothing underneath.

"Don't just stand there. Yes, you're both beautiful and slender and young and amazing. Now come and show me what kind of new delights you have dreamed up to amuse me today."

Preacher Mann dropped down on the Japanese floor bed, and then the two girls were on top of him pulling at his clothes, tickling him, undressing him. Preacher Mann laughed in surprise and with erotic anticipation.

CHAPTER 9

"Hey There, Mark Hardin!"

Mark watched the three men coming at him with baseball bats. Now this was more like it, the odds a little more even. One of the men ran faster than the others, faked one way, darted the other, then charged, swinging the bat at Mark's legs. Mark jumped the vicious arc of the bat and slammed both his feet into the attacker's chest, jolting him backward, making him drop the bat and curl up in agony and frustration on the sidewalk.

The other two kept coming. Mark grabbed the bat and met them. The bats cracked as they slashed at each other. Mark retreated up the alley to cut down on the number of spectators, and the two blacks grew more confident.

"Honkie bastard, you got about two minutes to live!" one of the men shouted.

Mark laughed, caught the man's blow with the bat on the solid part of his own, hitting the other bat just below the man's hands and shattering the Louisville slugger into a dozen pieces.

96

Mark charged in, taking advantage of the surprise, and, throwing his bat like a dart, heavy end first, sailed it six feet into the belly of the third black man. The victim went down with the wind knocked out of him.

From the corner of his eye Mark saw the man with the splintered bat reacting, seemingly turning away; then he executed a perfect spinning backkick, with his heel thudding into Mark's shoulder. The unexpected karate fighting move came as a surprise and toppled Mark to the ground, but he rolled and was on his feet again almost at once. He sent a kick of his own into the man's knee, then followed it with a crotch kick that put the black down and moaning.

Mark ran to the man who had the wind knocked out, threw him over his shoulder, and carried him out of the alley to his car just beyond. He put the man in the front seat, locked the door, and drove away before the other attackers could help their companion or follow him.

Mark drove high into the hills over Honolulu to the end of a road where there were no houses, and parked under some wild banana trees. The man was coming around, and when he came back to consciousness he looked over at a .45 aimed at his chest.

"You were lucky, motherfucker, just wild lucky," the black said. "One on one, I kill you."

"Then why couldn't you do it with three on one, creep? You really like working for that kiddie pornographic shit outfit?"

"It's a living."

"So is mugging little old ladies and ripping off tourists, but at least that's a little respectable." Mark waved the .45. "Get out your door, nice and slow. Walk over four steps and lie face down in the grass."

"You jiving me?"

"You want a .45 barrel across the side of your black skull?"

"You not jiving me." The youth got out slowly, making no mistakes, as Mark slid over and followed him. When he was flat on the ground, Mark tugged a plastic riot cuff strip around his ankles, binding them together.

"Roll over and sit up, then put your hands behind your back," Mark instructed. The man did and Mark tightened another riot cuff on the crossed wrists. The plastic wouldn't come off until it was cut with a knife.

"Now, who do you work for?" Mark asked.

The black snorted. "I won't tell you one damn word. You won't lay a hand on me."

Mark backhanded him hard, the black face swinging around in spite of the tightened neck muscles.

"Blackie, I'm from Chicago. We eat shit like you for breakfast. Uncle Harry is expanding, and he wants Hawaii, so he can mix his business with pleasure. You dig? So first he hits the porn because you cats are so soft. That means tough for your black ass. I'd just as soon put about three new holes in that skull of yours as look at it. For starters I'm from Georgia and I don't like niggers. So you want to stay healthy, you give when I ask."

The black man laughed. "Shit. That is the worst imitation of a mobster I've ever heard. Where you pick up that jive?"

The open palm of Mark's right hand swung, cracking the man's cheek, rolling him into the grass to one side.

Mark unstrapped the plastic pack on his leg and took out his persuasion kit. It held a two-cubic-centimeter hypodermic syringe and six small plastic ampules of various fluids.

"Hey, what the hell is that?"

"I'm trying to decide. I have curare here, a deadly poison, and with it you have about two minutes to live

98

after I inject it. Or there's the yellow one that's plain old novocaine. On a particularly stupid person I can make him think I've killed a finger or a whole hand. But you're too dumb; it wouldn't work on you. Then we have the old reliable, sodium pentothal."

"Hey, that's truth serum. You can't use that on me, that's illegal."

"Well fancy that. Illegal? So is decapitating a honkie with a baseball bat."

Mark took out the ampule with truth serum in it, unsealed it from its protective plastic wrap, and then pulled the fluid from the container, drawing it in through the needle.

"I understand the headache is terrible after you wake up from this stuff. Two solid days, no sleep, no letup, just a constant pain. You don't have to get this headache. Just tell me who you work for, where the office is, and where you get the books you distribute. You get a bonus for telling me where the presses are that print this stuff."

"Go to hell, you white bastard."

Mark rammed the needle into his upper arm and shot the fluid in. It was enough to make the black man groggy after a few minutes, but not unconscious. Depending on bulk, some people went farther under than others. But it also had the strange effect on the mind of releasing all inhibitions, and turning the victim into a cooperative subject for questions. Still the questions had to be phrased simply, and the movement from subject to subject had to be done slowly, so it didn't confuse the patient.

Mark waited until the drug had taken effect, and then began.

"What's your name?"

"My name? Willy Washington."

"Right, Willy. Where do you live?"

"In a house."

"What's the address?"

"At 1212 Lalani Court."

"How many of you live there?"

"Five."

Mark went over and over the same basic questioning often, and put in a vital question he wanted answered, but after the drug began wearing off almost an hour later, he still had learned very little. He was convinced it was because the man knew little about the operation. Mark had the address of the Island Periodical Distributors, the outfit Willy worked for. All they handled was *Life Child*, and only four other men worked there. They had five trucks and distributed the magazines five days a week.

Willy Washington didn't know where the magazines came from. He said an unmarked truck delivered them once a month to their dock.

Period. End of report.

Mark drove back downtown and left Washington in a parking lot where he cut off the plastic riot cuffs. Washington was still groggy but beginning to shout obscenities at Mark. He would live.

The next stop was Island Periodicals. Nobody was there. The small building was dark, and no one came to the door. It was in half of a building that also housed a printing press, and an instant-printing Xerox machine. This printing outfit could have nothing to do with Preacher Mann.

Mark drove past the Tipped Canoe Club and wondered if he should go in and put the squeeze on Tom Kim. He decided not now, not in the middle of the day. Later, when he might catch Mr. Kim alone, or on his

100

way home. That would be a better time to talk to him, especially if the two giant Chinese were not around.

If that didn't produce, he'd have to try another angle he'd been thinking of. Printing for the quality and quantity shown by the *Life Child* material would require a big supply of paper, art materials, inks, workers, a press, much equipment. Mark was sure that none of that came air express COD. He would take a look at the big printers on the island and print-equipment suppliers tomorrow.

Mark felt frustrated. There was nothing he could do right then. Nothing he could think of that would advance his project. He drove toward Waikiki, parked, and walked along the famous surf, getting white sand in his shoes, past the fantastic Sheraton Waikiki Hotel, the Royal Hawaiian, the Moana-Surfrider. Each was almost a whole community in itself. It would be an easy life to put on some trunks, rent a surfboard, and try his hand at the waves. Then soak up the sun and rest and relax for about a year. When he retired, maybe he would come to Hawaii. Mark sat on a cement bench for a while, staring at the tourists, then walked into the Royal Hawaiian Hotel's patios and paths and through the luxurious accommodations on his way back to his car.

He would go to his hotel, grab a quick lunch, then take a nap, and be ready to go as soon as it got dark again and he could go and follow Mr. Kim.

Mark parked in the White Sands Hotel's "Guests Only" lot, showed the lot boy his room key, and went into the lobby. He never checked at the desk because no one knew he was there so there could be no messages. There better *not* be any messages!

He had just passed the desk heading for the elevators when he saw someone jump up from a chair in the lobby. Mark always watched for sudden movements, unusual sounds, anything that might precede an attack. He held himself alert as he moved across the rest of the lobby. He was only a few feet from the elevator when he felt—more than heard—the running feet behind him. He stepped quickly to his left and felt someone brush past him.

"Hey, Mark! For Christ's sake, it is you! You no-good jungle rat! Hey, Mark Hardin!"

Mark stopped and turned slowly, wanting desperately to be holding the comforting .45 from his belt holster. Somebody had nailed him down good, but who could it be way out here?

CHAPTER 10

Headhunters Team Up Again

"Hey, Sergeant Hardin. It's okay, it's me, Uchi, Corporal Takayama. You okay, Sarge? For a minute there I thought for sure you were going to whirl around and come down on me with an M-14 blasting the hell out of me just like we used to do to them Cong in 'Nam."

Mark's face relaxed, his jaw sagged in surprise, and he took two steps back and held out his hand. *It was Uchi*, one of the guys from 'Nam he had gone out on dozens of patrols with, and who had helped form one of the best seven-man headhunter teams he'd ever put together.

"Uchi, you little sonofabitch! Damn but it's good to see you! Must be seven, eight years now, maybe more. What are you doing in Hawaii?"

"I live here, remember? Christ, Sarge, but you looked shell-shocked when I came up behind you. I thought I was gonna buy it right here. Glad you didn't have a weapon in your hand at that time." He laughed. "Shit, and I thought I was the one half hung out today.

Come on, Sarge, I think you need a good stiff drink about now."

Mark tried to relax. The shock of hearing his real name called out behind him, the running feet, the sudden movement, all were more than enough to trigger a dozen reactions from him. Uchi was right. If he had been holding a weapon in his hand he would have reacted, not thought, just reacted, and he would have spun around ready to fire.

Mark concentrated on the drink, not sure what it was; but it came in a pint-sized long-stemmed glass and had three kinds of fruit in it, and something else with a real wallop. Mark sipped at it and shook his head.

"You just about flipped me out when you yelled that way, Uchi. I can't really explain it, but I'd appreciate it if you didn't use that name anymore."

"Yeah, it figures. Hell, you must be undercover. I should have guessed. Hey, hope I didn't blow your cover or anything. Uchi belted down half the drink.

"Chopsticks, tell me how it's gone since you got out. What are you doing now?"

"Doing? Hell, I'm working for my cousin driving a hack—well almost a hack. I drive a Diamond Head Sightseeing Minibus, a little fourteen-passenger Ford van bus. I run a one-way-around-the-island tour. It's a bore, but at least I don't have anybody looking over my shoulder, yelling at me." He pulled on the drink. "Besides, it's the only Goddamned job I been able to hold since I got out." He put down the glass and it jiggled as he let go of it on the bar. Uchi glanced up at Mark.

"Yeah, I know, Sarge. My nerves are shot. Hell, they been that way for longer than you want to know. Hey, remember that trip we took hunting that little Cong general who was raising hell around Tam Quang? We waded into his headquarters, blew away half his staff and then got him in his own private whorehouse. That was the last run I remember going on with you. After that things went right into the old honey bucket.

"I got shot up and pulled some hospital time. Ever since then I've been bouncing off the walls day and night." He looked up and Mark saw a despair that shocked him.

"Mark, they didn't feed us guys any of those experimental drugs, did they? I heard about that black guy in Germany they gave acid to, you know LSD. They never even told the poor sonofabitch. He's still falling flat on his face thirty years later and he doesn't know why."

"Uchi, are you on disability? The country owes you, Uchi. You were the best damn sideman in the shooting business. I know a guy in Washington who gets things done, Justice Department. He'll get you disability for as long as you need it. What's your home address, somewhere you can always be reached?"

Uchi gave Mark his mother's address. Mark memorized it, then watched his old friend. He was twenty pounds lighter than he had been, which brought him down to about one hundred and thirty. He wasn't a big man at five-feet-eight, but now he was as skinny as a bamboo shoot. Uchi's eyes never held Mark's for long. He moved in the booth at the little bar in Mark's hotel.

"Sarge, I picked up a batch of people for a short tour this morning here at your hotel, and I thought I saw you, but I figured it couldn't be you. I decided to come back and check it out. You know, just wait around and see if you really did show. Then there you were."

"What about your art, Uchi? You still drawing? Seemed to me you were always sketching when we were in 'Nam. You'd draw with pencils or ball-point or charcoal and send them all home. You ever do anything with them?"

"Hell, nobody wants to look at 'Nam pictures. That was the most unpopular war we ever fought and lost, remember? Anyway, I don't have the patience to hold a brush anymore, or charcoal."

"You're a natural, Uchi. What about your family? I thought Japanese families were closely knit, strong. Haven't your people helped you?"

Uchi laughed and finished the drink. "That's the only way I could have held six jobs in three years. When your relatives won't even keep you on the payroll, you know damn well that you're in one hell of a mess."

"Who's your family's head man—dai ichi, you used to call him?"

"You remember that?" Uchi shrugged. "Kono Takayama, old Kono himself. Hawaiian name. Japanese blood thicker than Tokyo smog."

Mark moved away from it. He talked about the Islands, but soon Uchi came back to a subject that bothered him.

"Hey, Mark. Why you so jumpy? You aren't now, but when I called out your name you froze up like a berg, and I knew you were going to whirl and give me an automatic blast. What the hell are you doing now, anyway?"

Mark had been thinking what he could tell Uchi. He had depended on this man dozens of times, bet his life on the wiry little Japanese. Uchi had given Mark covering fire; he had taken a flank and blasted their way out. He had come up beside Mark and shot Cong gunmen out of trees and bushes and buildings more times than either of them could count. Mark knew he could trust Uchi Takayama with his life now as well, but he hesitated.

Dozens of times in the past few years people who

had touched Mark's life, sometimes only for an hour or two, became captives and pawns in this game, and most of them died in the process. Mark didn't want to endanger Uchi again.

Mark sipped his drink, then opened his jacket so Uchi could see the .45 in his clip-on holster.

Uchi lifted his brows and sucked in a breath.

"You were right, Uchi. I am undercover." He laughed softly. "But I'm so damn far undercover that nobody knows it. I'm not a cop. I'm not with any local, state, or federal organization. I'm what you might call a free-lancer."

"You pick the job you want?"

"True, Uchi, but I don't hire out. I'm not a gun for sale. Or an investigator for hire. I work for myself, matter of fact. Is that enough for you?"

Uchi shook his head. A new thread of interest came into his eyes. "Hey, man, you're just getting me curious. You rich now or something? You work for yourself; then who picks up the tab? I mean I worry about the tab; I'm always short on cash."

Mark stared at him, then grabbed the check. "Room 404. Meet me up there in ten minutes." Without another word, Mark got out of the booth, paid the bill, walked out of the bar and up to his room.

Uchi knocked on the door right on schedule and went inside quickly. He tossed a New York Yankees baseball cap on the bed and frowned at Mark.

"You in some kind of trouble? Level with me, man. We been in lots worse holes than this could be."

"You know I was with CIC for a while in 'Nam. Sniffed out a black market you wouldn't believe and I leaked it to the press. The army brass didn't like that and I had a run-in with some hard cases who thought they had beaten me to death. But I survived and later got a

107

discharge. Now I'm as good as new, but it left a bad taste in my mouth for crooks of any kind.

"So, now I look for a particularly rotten spot and move in and see if I can clean it up a little. I'm not too particular about doing things legally, and if some shithead needs to be wasted he sometimes meets a sudden end. So the FBI and about thirty police departments have "wanted" notices out on me, only they don't know my name and I aim to keep it that way."

"So you're a kind of a cop without a badge?"

"Something like that."

"And you're in town digging into some problem. Then I barge in and call your name in a lobby full of people and I might have blown your cover, got you killed or maybe arrested. Hey, I'm a real buddy. Why didn't I just take out an ad and let everybody know you're in town?"

Mark grinned. "It isn't that critical. And I still owe you about a dozen from 'Nam."

"No more thn I owe you, buddy. We were a damned good team."

"The best, Uchi. Only the Goddamned best!"

"Hey, remember the time we had to carry that little slope colonel on our backs because he refused to walk? Said he'd reather die where he sat, even tried to do the job himself? Damn but he was a heavy bastard. As I remember you did most of the carrying."

Mark saw the fire come back into Uchi's eyes as he talked about the good old days. When there had been excitement, action, and danger in his life.

"Is it a little dull for you around here, now, Uchi?"

"Dull? Hell, it's worse than that. But nobody is trying to kill me. But then, I'm not shooting at anybody either. I guess maybe that might be part of it. Dull and boring, and I'm still a little . . ."

108

"Yeah, buddy, I know. How about teaming up with me for a few days? I need a driver who knows how to handle a .45, and knows this crazy town. I get lost after two or three blocks. What's this Mauka and Makai jazz?"

Uchi laughed. "Easy. Mauka means toward the mountains, or generally north; Makai means seaward, or usually south." He looked up at Mark. "You really mean that, my helping out? I can get off a few days from this job with no damn sweat."

Mark drew the .45 from his waist and tossed it to Uchi. The thin Japanese man caught the weapon and a second later had it trained on the lampshade.

"Hell, Uchi, you've slowed down. You used to be able to catch it one-handed with your finger already in the trigger guard." They both laughed. "Yes, Uchi, I need you. Time is getting short and I've got some digging to do. How about tomorrow morning at 8:30. I'll meet you in the parking lot. I've got a rented blue Pinto." Mark paused. "Hey, Chopsticks, you married?"

Uchi shook his head.

Mark filled him in on the mission, showed him the magazine and told him what had happened up to then.

"So I want to find out where these things are printed and move in and roust the place, burn it down, blow it up, anyway that works."

"Sounds like old times. Count me in."

"It's three hundred a day for driving and combat pay. Hope you don't mind getting shot at. It could happen."

Uchi snorted. "I've been shot at so many times before, a few more won't matter. I'll be there in the morning."

Mark held up his hand. "Oh, and bring a sketch pad

109

with you. We may find a face we want to remember."

"Yeah, sure."

Uchi was waiting beside Mark's Pinto when he went out the next morning at 8:30.

"Had breakfast?" Mark asked.

"Of course, rice and unhatched baby chicks in soy sauce. Where to?"

Mark gave him the address of the largest printer-lithographer in the islands, Honolulu Printing. Mark had on his executive suit and vest, carried a plastic zipper case with two copies of *Life Child* inside. They drove to the firm and Mark got out, leaving Uchi in the car. He went through two secretaries before he got to the vice-president in charge of production.

Mark showed his Justice Department ID, explaining that he was on an undercover mission from Washington, and asked if the man knew who had printed the *Life Child* magazines.

At first the executive recoiled from the pedophile publications; then he studied them from a printing-technique angle.

"First, Mr. Johnson, we didn't print these. We wouldn't touch this sort of filth. But it *is* a good print job. It is professionally done, quality presswork. But I assure you no legitimate printer in the Islands would touch it. I know all the men that run the big printing houses, and they simply would not do this kind of work. It must be some outlaw firm. But that would be hard because of the press. It takes an expensive web offset press to print a magazine like this, and they cost hundreds of thousands of dollars."

"And you don't know any of the established firms here who might take on this job"

"I'm sure they wouldn't."

110

"What about printers, pressmen. Have you had any top-level journeymen printers quit in the past several months, a year or so?"

"We get very little turnover now. Not like in the old days. But there was one man we were sorry to lose, Larston Ohura. Damn good man. Wouldn't say what he was going to do. He was the best color pressman in the Islands, bar none."

"Would you have his last known address? This will be confidential government business. He'll never know where we got it. This is all pretty much routine anyway."

Mark got the address and went back to the car. They visited the other three top printing outfits in the city and got much the same story. Legitimate printers wouldn't produce the magazines. Two of the other printers had let go good-quality pressmen, but one of them went to Los Angeles and the other opened up his own small shop. Dead end there. One of the men said good printers were easy to find. Put an ad in the Los Angeles *Times* and you could have a dozen phone calls the next day.

It was almost noon when Mark came out of the last place. The man who ran it was Chinese, and became angry when he saw the magazine. He wasn't aware things like that existed, he said.

Back in the car, Mark showed Uchi the address he had on the one printer, Larston Ohura.

"Hey, man. That's a good address. Up in the Honolulu hills. There some big sombitching mansions up there. Not all of them, but some beauties. I used to take a tour through there to kill a little time when I was early on my schedule."

"Take me on your tour, Uchi. Let's see if we can talk to this guy Larston Ohura."

111

"Careful, he sounds like he's a damned Jap." They both laughed.

Uchi drove the rented Pinto up the streets into the heights. He wound around for ten minutes before he found the street he wanted, and then came to an abrupt stop. There was a guard box in the middle of the narrow street, and a uniformed man with a two-way radio stood there. Mark noted he also had a pistol on his hip and the usual police leathers. He came out to talk to them and smiled. He was Oriental, a mixture of something, but mostly Chinese.

"Good afternoon, gentlemen, do you have an entry pass?"

"Pass?" Uchi said. "We're just going to see a friend up the street a ways. What's this, some kind of a toll road?"

"Not really, sir," the guard said. He kept smiling. "You see, some years ago the city refused to fix up the road here, so the residents got together and found that this street had never been formally vacated and given to the city. So they paved it, put up notices that it was a private road, and by the time the city tried to do anything about it, the street was ruled legally private. So now we have a security gate here, and we keep out anyone not having business in this area."

"Sounds like you've used that spiel before, man," Uchi said. "All we want to do is go in and see a friend. Call him. Tell him Uchi is here."

The guard took Ohura's name and went in the little square guardhouse. In a few moments he was back.

"Sorry, there's no answer at Mr. Ohura's number. Next time phone ahead and get him to leave a clearance for you at the gate. That's all it takes."

"No way we can go see him?" Uchi asked.

"Especially when he's not at home."

112

"Yeah, man," Uchi said and turned the car around and drove away.

"Was he conning me, Uchi?" Mark asked.

"I'm not sure. That damn gate wasn't there three years ago, I know that. There is a Japanese showplace around here somewhere that I used to drive past. But this could be a legit deal. Most of the land in the Islands is owned by maybe a dozen huge corporations. The old missionary descendants. You buy a house here and you get a leasehold, not a freehold. You're just leasing the land from the corporation but you own the house. So the corporation might have closed up the street. Especially way up here."

"So what do we do now?" Mark asked, thinking out loud. "We try to phone Ohura when he gets home. Maybe he's working. If he's there, we go back and do a little bit of line-crossing."

Uchi's eyes snapped. "Hey, you mean we creep and crawl, go through that little guard post like that joker was sleeping?"

"The same. Just like old times, Uchi. Only now we don't kill anybody going in or coming out. Makes it a lot tougher."

"Oh, yeah, now you're talking! Listen, until then, you mainlander, how about Uchi, local native guide, giving you the special fifteen-cent tour of Bishop Museum? Now, Mr. Hardin, we are about to enter one of the most important natural history museums in the Pacific, which makes the world of the early Polynesian settlers come alive. You will see . . ."

CHAPTER 11

One Small, Scared Printer

By the time the soft, golden Hawaiian sun had slid near the Pacific Ocean, Mark and Uchi were sitting in the rented Pinto high in the hills in back of Honolulu. Uchi had stopped at a small restaurant owned by one of his many uncles, and where he had worked for a while, and came out with a basket of food. He then drove into the hills where they could eat and watch the sunset at the same time.

The food basket wasn't your usual McDonald's take-out, he told Mark. They had a salty noodle soup, then fried octopus in spicy cocktail sauce, a plastic tub of sashimi, thinly sliced raw fish, cooked seaweed greens, and whole fried oysters marinated in soy sauce. Mark ate some of everything, even the raw fish, but his favorite was the sweet slabs of rice-flour bread.

"Not bad for a handout, huh, Sarge," Uchi said grinning.

"It's one helluva lot better than C-ration ham and lima beans," Mark said and they laughed, remembering how many times they had eaten from the little C-ration cans.

Darkness came slowly. They talked about old times, and Mark saw a growing confidence returning to his friend. His step was quicker, his glance penetrating, his decisions quick, firm.

When it was fully dark they drove two blocks from the gate and left the Pinto. Mark had on his black long-sleeved T-shirt and his tight black pants. Uchi wore dark-blue pants and shirt. They came at the gate from each side, sliding through bushes and shrubbery around the middle-income-type houses until they were within thirty feet of the edge of the forbidden street.

One was on each side and they signaled when they were ready. The guard sat on a high stool inside the lighted cubicle reading a magazine. Any small distraction should do the trick. Uchi had provided the method earlier that afternoon when they stopped at a fireworks store.

Mark took out a cigarette lighter, shielded it, and lit the twisted-together fuses of three cherry bomb firecrackers. When they spurted into fire, he threw them over the fence and inside the protected area. A moment later one exploded with a resounding bang that made Mark think of a .38 pistol going off. The other two were blown some distance away by the early fuse blast of the first and went off in quick succession.

The guard dropped his magazine and surged out of the guardhouse on the run, charging inside the fence toward the spot where the small explosions had sounded. As he ran into the darkness Mark and Uchi rose from their hiding places, charged through the gate, and sprinted out of the spotlights to the shrubs on the other side of the fence in the side yard of the house just past the gate.

115

A moment later the guard's flashlight came on, and he shone it in the bushes on the far side of the gate looking for the invader. Mark and Uchi moved away from him through the shrubs and soon went to the sidewalk and strolled along in what looked to be an ordinary suburban street with houses on both sides.

Uchi grinned. "That gate was a piece of cake."

"True. Hope it's as easy to get out. What's the address?"

"Eleven fifteen, about a dozen houses more along on this side of the street," Uchi said. "Ohura, he must be Japanese, but how did he get a crazy first name like Larston?"

They found the address and rang the bell. The man who turned on the light and came to the door was an inch shorter than Uchi, about ten years older, and definitely Japanese.

Uchi chattered with him in their native language for a while, and then the man stepped back and motioned to them.

"Please come in, Mr. Johnson. I understand that you want to talk with me about printing?"

"Yes, sir. We're interested."

"Can I get you a drink? Some hot sake perhaps?"

Mark and Uchi nodded and Mr. Ohura brought a long green bottle with the potent fermented rice wine. The delicate Oriental handleless cups were filled and passed around.

"Mr. Ohura, we know that you're a printer. We wonder where you're working right now?"

"Are you police?" he asked. "I know there is nothing illegal in what I'm doing, but I'm not proud of it. I'm working for a secretive group and that's all I think I should say. How did you get through the gate?"

"Mr. Ohura, we know you don't work for any of the

116

larger printers in town. We're wondering who you work for now?" Mark took out his false identification from the Justice Department and showed it to the man, who began to tremble.

"My work is not illegal, I tell you. You have no right . . ." He sighed. "I'm sorry. I shouldn't have yelled at you that way. But I am under much pressure here. I don't even like what I'm doing. But I have a wife and two children! They must be provided for and protected. . . ."

"Mr. Ohura, had your employer threatened your family?"

"Yes, of course, that's why I stay."

"Do you work for Multimedia, Inc.?"

"I've never heard of that name."

"Mr. Ohura, do you work printing a magazine called *Life Child?*"

The Japanese man gasped, then put his hands over his face and bent low on the couch.

Uchi looked at Mark and nodded.

"Mr. Ohura, we are not here to arrest you, or to harm you in any way. We're trying to find out all we can about the people who publish this material. We're trying to stop them. Will you help me?"

"Yes. If you'll help me and my family to get out of here. If we can leave tonight. These madmen have made my wife and my children pose for those disgusting pictures. It is almost more than they can stand. My wife has bad dreams. The children are terrified. We must leave tonight!"

"How could we do that?"

"I'll call my supervisor. Tell him that I must talk to him tonight. If he comes, we can use him as a hostage to get through the gate. I don't have a gun, they don't allow us any in the compound. . . ."

Mark showed him the .45 from his belt.

"Good! Excellent! That will give us the power we need. I have a car. We all can ride in it."

"Do you know who runs the business, Mr. Ohura? Is it a big black man?"

"Yes, the evil one himself. I have seen him. He's an angry man, a bad one. He's a devil. They call him Preacher Mann."

Mark smiled grimly. "Yes, that's the man I'm hunting. We'll get you out of here; then you tell us everything you know about this outfit. We want to know where the headquarters is, where they print the things, where they ship from, and everything you know about them."

"Gladly, Mr. Johnson. First let me talk to my wife, and get her ready. We can come back for our things later. We just want to get away!"

He was gone only five minutes and returned with a tiny Japanese woman with a flat, frightened face and black eyes.

Uchi bowed to her and spoke rapidly in Japanese. She answered and her fear seemed to subside a little.

"Hello, Mrs. Ohura," Mark said. "Please do not worry. We are here to help you any way we can."

"Those awful men! Please take us away from here."

"We will, Mrs. Ohura. Just as soon as we can. You go get the children ready to travel."

She bowed and hurried away. Mark turned to Mr. Ohura. "You said you'd call someone to be a hostage. Why can't we just drive through the gate?"

"We need a pass to get out of here. There are huge steel spikes that rise up out of the street automatically whenever a car drives up from the inside. It's worked on a pressure relay system. The guard has to inspect the

118

car and examine your exit order before he will switch the spikes down."

"Couldn't we just capture the guard, go inside and push the button ourselves to lower the spikes?" Uchi asked.

Ohura shook his head. "No, no. There is a combination needed that he punches up on a little computer panel to unlock the system and pull the spikes down. Only the guard knows the combination of numbers that must be used. The numbers change three times a day. We need that hostage. When my supervisor comes he'll be in his own car and probably with a driver. The supervisors never come out here alone at night anymore. We'll have to capture him first."

"Call him," Mark said. "Uchi and I will be outside waiting and hidden. They'll never know what hit them."

"Oh, I don't want anyone hurt!"

"Don't worry, we're not here to hurt people," Mark said. "What we want to do is get you out, then we can talk."

Mr. Ohura went to the phone and Mark and Uchi slipped outside through the back door and looked over the front of the house. If the supervisor were smart, or a little uneasy, the car would come to the curb in front of the house, ready for a fast getaway. There was no good cover out there. But there would be the normal blind spots behind the car. Mark took the near side in the shrubs. He wasn't sure which way the car would come, but it figured to come from the direction they had walked in. Uchi was across the street. Quickly both were out of sight and waiting.

It was ten minutes before a car drove up, coming the way Mark guessed it would. It stopped, the lights went off, then the horn sounded twice. Ohura's front door opened, the porch light was off, and he stepped out, walked to the car and bent down to talk through the front driver's-side window.

By the time Ohura got there, Mark had slid along the rear fender of the car, his .45 in his hand. He saw the window roll down and the man in the passenger side start to talk. Uchi moved up on the driver's side and signaled. Mark pushed Ohura aside and held the .45 trained on the man's head who sat in the car.

"Don't move, either of you or you're both dead. Hands on the wheel, driver!" Mark spoke the last sharply. He saw Uchi reach in and take the keys from the ignition, then open the far door. Mark opened the door on his side.

"Outside, both of you, and no mistakes, I'd just as soon shoot you both as look at you."

The passenger in the car was black, about thirty, and Mark's size. The other man was a small Chinese who did exactly as he was told. They took the men inside the house through the dark back door, where Uchi tied their hands behind them.

The black man spoke for the first time. "You're a dead man, Ohura. I left a report where I was coming and why. You're a dead man."

"Don't count on it, Zara," Ohura said. "Don't count on anything, except maybe trying to stay alive yourself. I never knew until now how much I hate you people and what you're doing."

"You're a dead man, you and your family, and these two honkie-bastard helpers."

Mark ignored him. "Get your family in your car," Mark told Ohura. "We may not have much time."

Mrs. Ohura and her two children, a boy about ten and a girl of eight, quickly went into the garage and got into the rear seat of a two-year-old Ford wagon. Uchi

120

tied up the Chinese and told him someone would find him soon, not to worry. Zara was led out the side door and put in the front seat on the passenger's side next to the window. Mark sat between him and the driver, and Uchi squeezed in the back seat.

"Zara, listen to me," Mark said. "You know who I am?"

Zara nodded.

"Then you know I'd just as soon slice off your head as let you live. You buy your worthless life by doing exactly as I tell you. You dig?"

Zara nodded.

"We're driving to the gate. You tell the guard the right words to get us through or you and the guard are both dead and we'll still get through by leaving the car and running out. Is that all perfectly clear in that pedophilic-type mind of yours?"

"Yeah, yeah. Let's get on with it."

Mark wondered for a minute if the man were too eager for them to be started. But he could have set up nothing to stop them. He didn't know what the problem was before he arrived. Mark's only worry was if the man were wearing a voice transmitting device and they were coming in loud and clear on some receiver. He'd have to risk that. Mark told everyone to be quiet and they left, Mark's .45 pushed into Zara's ribs.

It was only three blocks to the gate, which was still brightly lighted. Mark saw the steel spikes, two feet long, sharply pointed and stretching eight feet across the ten-foot-wide entrance. They rose automatically as the car drove up.

"Give him the right words!" Mark hissed as the car came to a stop and the guard moved to the driver's window.

"Guard, it's all right," Zara said loudly. "We have a

late-night shooting schedule for some pictures. And we're in a bit of a rush. Lower the protection."

The guard looked in and saw Zara; his face stiffened.

"Yes, sir, Mr. Zara. I didn't know it was you, sir. This isn't your usual outside car."

"I know that," Zara said impatiently. "Just open the gates."

The guard went into the cubicle and a moment later the metal spikes lowered. The guard waved and Ohura drove his car through the gate. They sped around a dozen corners and down the hills toward town. Mark wondered if he should keep Zara as a hostage to question later, but decided against it. He had Ohura, who would gladly tell him everything he knew.

Mark told Ohura to pull up and they let Zara out of the car, but Mark didn't untie his hands.

They drove away and Mark looked over at Ohura. "You're free now, you're outside. Where do you want to go?"

Ohura frowned, thinking it out. "Certainly not to any of my relatives. Preacher Mann knows all of them. It has to be a hotel, a small one somewhere that they wouldn't think to look." He kept driving.

"Now, Mr. Ohura, some questions. Do they print just the magazines here or are there other items?"

"Magazines, books, posters, sets of pictures, every filthy thing they can think of. All done right here, somewhere."

Mark frowned. "Somewhere? What do you mean?"

"I don't know where I've been working. Each morning a car picked me up. I was blindfolded and listened to the news on the radio, which was turned up loud. We drove to the printing plant. I timed it several days, and it was always a half-hour from my front door to the place where I worked. At the end of that time I was taken from the car, led down some steps and, when I was in my work area, the blindfold was taken off. They said I was still on probation and had to be blindfolded yet for six months. Lots of the other workers said the same thing happened to them."

"You're telling me you work some place but you don't even know where it's located?"

"Quite right. Should I have told you that before?"

Mark sighed. "It would have made it a lot easier. I could have worked over Zara and found out the exact spot."

"I'm sorry. I was thinking too much about myself, about my family. I should have known enough to tell you that quickly."

Mark waved his hand. "Don't worry about it; we'll get to it some other way."

"I do know that there is a magnificent Japanese mansion inside the gates. It's three stories tall, and built the traditional way with lots of rice-paper screens, and panels, and tatami floors. Laquered wood all over the place and outside fishponds."

"Hey, that's the one I remember," Uchi said from the backseat.

"But the big house is far too small to be where the printing is done," Ohura went on. "It's only a residence and a few offices. I went there for my first interview with Preacher Mann. That was before I knew what kind of printing they wanted me to do."

Mark nodded. So they had found Uchi's mansion, but a lot of good that did now. They needed a printing plant.

Mr. Ohura at last figured out where he wanted to go and turned the car toward Pearl City. He knew of a small hotel off the main roads where Preacher Mann wouldn't think of looking. He drove in and registered.

They had a pair of rooms on the second floor overlooking the parking lot. It didn't look like the safest place in the world, but Mark decided it would do.

Mark and Uchi said good-bye to Mr. Ohura and his family. Mark wrote down the number of the motel's phone, and then they caught a taxi back to his hotel. There Mark sent Uchi up the hill to reclaim their rented Pinto, told him to leave it in the parking lot, and he'd see him in the morning.

Mark stood at the window of his hotel room, looking over Honolulu's lights. He was little closer to finding the location of the printing plant now than he had been. There was nothing more he could do tonight. Tomorrow he would take the next step in his trackdown procedure. That one had to produce some results or he was left only with the prospect of going into the Japanese mansion and trying to wring the truth out of someone there. With the guards that Preacher Mann must have around the place, getting in might be a suicide mission, to say nothing of trying to get back out.

CHAPTER 12

Casualty Report: One Dead

Uchi had been sitting in the Pinto waiting for him when Mark went out at 8:00 the next morning. They drove straight to the lodging in Pearl City where the Ohuras were staying. It was a motel, and Mark and Uchi went to the second floor of the open-fronted building and knocked on the door. Mr. Ohura let them in. They had two rooms and were concerned about their personal things at the rented house.

Mark said that would have to wait.

"Mr. Ohura, do you remember any local firms that your former employer did business with? Where did they get their paper, ink? What about repair parts for the big press? Where did all of this material come from?"

Larston Ohura frowned as he thought about it. He paced for a moment.

"I wondered where they bought things too. That was because most of the labels were torn off things we got. But I saw one name several times. It was on special press parts and some unusual inks we got from Waikiki

Printing Supplies. Some of the things we needed quickly so we could meet deadlines. Whoever brought the items forgot to tear off the supplier's name. But that's the only one I can remember. The paper was all taken care of by someone else. But I did see that Waikiki name several times."

"You're sure, positive?"

"Yes, absolutely. I couldn't swear where anything else came from, though, or where it went. I do remember seeing a lot of electric trucks running around. Big ones, what we used to call two-ton trucks, with the big van body on them, twenty feet long. They backed right into loading docks in the buildings."

"Any more idea about where the printing plant could be? Did you hear any outside sounds, surf, wind, planes?"

"Not a thing, sorry. And none of these buildings had any windows. That always seemed strange to me. Not a single window."

Mark thanked him, said they'd get him back to his rented house as soon as they could, and then they walked back to the Pinto. For a minute Mark wished Ohura had picked a hiding place with greater security. Anyone could drive up here, throw one hand grenade through the front window, and could wipe out the whole family. Mark decided there was no way Preacher could have followed him here. So it wasn't anything to worry about.

Mark had put on his executive three-piece suit that morning, and now they drove back to downtown Honolulu to the White Sands Hotel, where Mark stopped to get his briefcase. He ran back to the car, opened the briefcase, and took out the hotel telephone book. He used it to look up the address of the Waikiki Printing Supplies firm.

It wasn't far from the hotel, and when they went inside a secretary referred them to Red O'Brien in the customer-supply department.

O'Brien had red hair of course, a big grin and a bigger belly. He shook hands with them both. "I been around here longer than the damned menehunes. If there is something about this place I don't know, it's because nobody ever asked."

"You're our man then," Mark said. "I'm looking for a printer; I've forgotten the outfit's name and I don't recognize it in the damned yellow pages. They have a big rotary web job—I don't even know which make, but it's a big, expensive son of a gun—for printing magazines. They need supplies and small parts and repair stuff. Can you give me the names of three or four outfits in town you sell that kind of material to?"

"Sure can," O'Brien said. He rattled off the names of the four biggest printers in town.

"That's my problem," Marks aid. "It's none of those. It must be some private press, or some weirdo in an old airplane hangar somewhere. Have you had any strange names come up in your supply work that didn't quite mesh with what seemed logical? Like some little outfit ordering parts for a big press?"

The man stopped and scratched his thinning red hair. He looked like he enjoyed his work, Mark thought, but he was puzzled now. At last he nodded. "Yeah, maybe. I might have something. Any particular part of town?"

"Not sure, could be anywhere."

"I've got three of them. Outfits I never heard of before a couple of years ago. And still don't hear much from them. I mean in the business; must not be doing very well. But they all must have sophisticated equipment from the supplies and gear they get—or got. One is Mid Pacific Media, another one is Lehua Printing, and the last one is Islands Graphics Research. I don't know much about any of them, and it might just be a wild wahine chase, but like I say, a little wild chasing around never hurt nobody."

Mark thanked him and they went out to the car where Mark fished out the phone book and they found the addresses for all three.

The first one, Mid Pacific Media was closed, with a sheriff's big padlock on the door, and a notice of a sheriff's sale of assets two weeks away posted in the window.

Lehua Printing was a small outfit in the area out near Pearl City, but they concentrated on speedy print, Xeroxing, and wedding invitations. The last one was Islands Graphics Research, Inc. Uchi found it on the edge of the Honolulu hills less than a mile from where they had taken the road up to the guarded gate. They tracked down the right number at the end of a gravel street, an unpainted building backed up against a bluff and with little except green rocky outgrowths above it. The building was about a hundred feet long and forty wide, not in good repair, but had a new chain link fence around it with a locked gate. There were no cars inside, and the place looked deserted.

Mark got out and tried the gate, where he found a buzzer which he pushed. Over the buzzer was a sign: CLOSED. FOR FURTHER INFORMATION CALL 414-6464. Mark looked at the place again, then got back in the car.

"Notice anything unusual about this setup?" Mark asked Uchi.

"It's old, kind of run down, needs painting and has a new fence. What else?"

"It has three expensive TV camera monitors covering the side door, the front door, and the gate. I have a feeling I've just been on TV."

"Doesn't prove a thing. Lots of businesses are putting in cameras now. They say it's cheaper than renting a German shepherd watchdog."

"Let's find a phone."

Two blocks down Mark used a telephone and got a busy signal when he called the Island Graphics number. He tried it four times and each call resulted in a busy buzz.

Back in the car, Mark sat there trying to think it through. Maybe Ohura knew this name. It could ring a bell with him, and then they could dig into it more. Mark went back to the phone, and called the Ohura's motel. The phone rang five times before someone picked it up.

"Look, I can't talk now. We've had a hell of a thing happen here. Some guy got himself killed. Just shot up terrible and knifed. Now don't call back." The phone dropped on the cradle. Mark stared at it for thirty seconds, then ran for the Pinto.

"Pearl City, Uchi, and step on it. Our friend Ohura may not have found such a safe place as he thought."

A half-hour later they drove as close to the motel as they could. Police had blocked off the street and had uniformed men keeping the crowd on the sidewalk. Mark saw what he guessed were detectives going in and out of the second-floor rooms that the Ohuras had occupied.

"Hey, what happened here?" Mark asked a cop.

"A killing, that's all I know, mister."

"I've got some friends staying at this motel. How do I know if they're all right?"

The cop shrugged. A few moments later he pointed to a man coming across the parking lot with a TV camera-

129

man. "Ask that guy with the clipboard, when he gets here. He's a reporter; he should know the guy's name."

Mark stepped in front of the reporter as he tried to walk by, and the man scowled.

"Look, would you mind? I've got to get back to the studio."

"I would mind. You get past me as soon as you give me the name of the person who was killed and what happened."

The reporter scowled up at Mark. He was four inches shorter and not ready to get physical. "Hell, that's easy. His name was Larston Ohura. He got it with a knife, sliced up bad, probably bled to death. His wife and two kids are missing. Either they ran away scared or got kidnapped."

Mark turned away, his hands on his hips, anger and frustration masking his face. Uchi came up and pulled him back toward the car.

"Sarge, come on, snap out of it. We've had casualties before. He's a casualty; the fucking war ain't lost! Come on, get with it, or you and me might be the next turkey meat around here."

Mark got in the car, his fist coming down hard on the dash.

"How the hell did they do it? How did they find him?"

Uchi shrugged. "It could have been some kind of a bug. Maybe they got a bug on every suspect car inside the compound. Then if one of them gets out they'll know exactly where it goes, and when it comes back. Only this one didn't come back, so they knew where to go find it."

"A bug, I thought the supervisor might have some kind of a voice-sending mike on him. I never considered a tracer bug on the car. . . . Drive, Uchi. We bet-

130

ter move, or somebody might be zeroing in on us."
The car spun away from the curb and Uchi wheeled
back toward the downtown section.

Mark tried to put it all into the computer and it
didn't take long for him to come up with more trouble.
If they followed Ohura last night, they could have been
there this morning when he visited the printer. They
could also have followed Mark's Pinto when it went
back to the hotel. So Preacher Mann could know that
he was staying at the White Sands! He'd have to check
it out.

Mark told Uchi where to drive and leaned back
trying to see some sense in the whole thing. He was
saddened about Ohura. The man had done nothing. He
had brushed against Mark Hardin, the Penetrator, and
now he was dead. Mark didn't want to count the number of innocent persons who had died just because he
had spoken to them or talked to them.

He looked over at Uchi. That was one problem Uchi
was not going to have. He would cut loose from him
just as soon as he could. Uchi could take care of himself, but a thrown knife from the dark, or a sudden silenced .45 couldn't be guarded against. It would be a
lot less painful losing him now than finding him dead.

Mark watched as Uchi rolled the Pinto down the
street toward the hotel.

"Park in the lot. Drop me at the side door, and then
get to the far end of the parking lot and keep the motor
running. Watch for me. I'll come out the back door. We
may have to leave in a rush."

CHAPTER 13

Two Hit-Man Stakeout

Mark ran to the rear door of the White Sands Hotel and went to the stairs. He knew the killers would be waiting for him—now all he had to do was figure out where. The stairwell was a favorite spot. The stakeout could watch the room from the doorway to the stairs, or cover them if the victim tried to come up that way. Mark went up silently. Both stairwell doors looked out on his fourth-floor room, he remembered. The White Sands wasn't that big a place. No one was on the second-floor landing. The concrete stairwell had a painted steel railing, and a six-foot-square landing, then two slants of steps to the next floor. There was no way to see up until you got to the mid point on the second slant of steps.

Mark moved cautiously. His room being on the fourth, the watcher should be on his landing.

Mark crept up to the third, but found no one. On up. He edged up the steps so he could see the next landing, but there was no one there. He went to the door and cracked it so he could look down the hall. No one. Not a service worker, or maid, no phony cleaning man. Good. That cut down the odds.

Mark ran down the steps to the second floor, crossed through the hall, and went to the stairs at the other end of the building, working his way up silently. As he edged up from the third floor, he saw a man on the next landing. Mark hurried then, coming up in back of the black man, who had been looking out the cracked open door.

"Hey, man. You got a light? I'm all out of fire here and I need a smoke." The man turned, eyes bright with fear, then he relaxed a little and fumbled in his pocket. His jacket flipped back and Mark saw a weapon shoved in his waistband.

Mark grabbed the man and slammed him against the concrete stairwell wall. Mark jerked the weapon out of his belt and pushed it in front of the man's eyes.

"Okay, badass, who are you and why are you here? I'm hotel security and we don't like guys packing guns sneaking around our hotel and watching out stairwell doors. You got about two seconds to tell me who you are and what you're doing up here. And I want some answers, good, clean, and very quickly. You got a permit?"

"Hey, man. I was just going to my room; you got here just as I was on my way out."

"Yeah, what room number?"

"Room? Why, four-oh-four."

"Smart, yeah, you even got the floor right, but you could only remember the number of the room you're watching. You fucked badass; that's my room." Mark's lethal fingers dug into the man's throat, pushing hard, just short of bringing blood. "I can rip your throat open,

133

claw you so you'll bleed to death before you can scream for help. You want that, badass?"

Fear glazed the man's eyes. He struggled to control himself.

"Hey, no, man. I'm a hired hand. I do what they tell me."

"You work for Preacher Mann.

"Yeah. He wants you bad. You fucked him up good before. He says never again. He wants you turkey meat."

Mark brought the .38 down across the side of the man's head and he crumpled in Mark's arms. Mark put him on the concrete floor, tightened riot cuffs around his hands and ankles, and then pushed the .38 in his belt and slipped out the door into the hall.

There was no one in the corridor, but there probably was another man inside his room. Mark went up to the door whistling, jiggled the knob as he stood well past the door itself, along the wall on the doorknob side of the handle. Then he jiggled his key in the lock and turned it until it unlocked and the doorknob unlatched.

Four slugs came slapping through the door chest-high, making only a small splintering sound as they tore through the wood and embedded in the wall on the far side of the hall. Silencer being used inside—that figured.

Mark had unlatched the door before, and now the force of the four rounds swung the panel open slowly. Mark threw in a soft moan, and then hit the floor with his foot.

For a moment there was no other sound, no motion; then he heard two footsteps inside and the top of a black head appeared next to the door casing as someone moved forward to take a quick look into the hall past the door.

Before the eyes could clear the casing, Mark grabbed the Afro haircut with both hands and jerked the person across the hall slamming him into the wall, jolting the weapon from his hand. Mark grabbed the silenced .45 and dragged the black man back into his room.

No one else was inside. His room had been searched and torn apart. The killer on the floor groaned and tried to come to. Mark threw a pitcher of ice water on him and he sputtered and gasped and tried to sit up. Mark pushed him back to the floor with his half-boot and glared down at him.

"You son of a bitch, you tried to kill me! I should cut off your balls and laugh while you bleed to death."

The man glared back at Mark.

"Look, no sense your clamming up. I know Preacher Mann is your boss. I've got a few more questions to ask you." Mark put riot cuffs on the man's ankles, then on his wrists crossed behind his back. "Now, you all stay right there until I bring in your buddy," Mark said. He found the other hit man still in the stairwell where he had left him, picked up the big man, carried him to room 404, and dropped him on the floor.

"Two for the price of one. Now, we're going to play games. First a short shot of sodium pentothal to get your tongues loosened up." Mark reached for his hypodermic pack and scowled. He had used the truth serum. He had considered carrying extra sets of the chemical packs with him, but he didn't have any now. His one dose was used and he needed two more. He knew he would never get much out of this pair without it. They were pros. He might get a little if he started slicing them up and letting them bleed, but that wasn't his style. And truth serum wasn't exactly the sort of thing you walked in and ordered over the drugstore counter. He looked at his door. Four neat holes showed

135

from this side. But there were splinters outside. Some maid or maintenance man was going to get curious soon. And Preacher Mann might have another hit squad as a backup coming up here at any second.

Mark grabbed his suitcase and dumped everything in that he had taken out, which wasn't much. Then he carried both men into the bathroom and put them in the tub. After that he called the lobby and told them he was checking out, to get his bill ready and send up a bellboy for his bags.

Mark had his suitcases ready and the door open wide when the boy came so he woudn't see the splinters. Mark waved him on ahead as he went out with the bag, and closed the door himself. So far, so good. At the desk he paid and checked out, then stopped at the last phone booth nearest the back door.

He called the police and told them there were two hit men tied up in room 404 along with the silenced .45 weapon that had been used to kill Larston Ohura. They should get over there right away. Mark hung up when they asked his name and went out the rear entrance.

Uchi had moved so he would have a quick shot at the back door, and now gunned the Pinto into position as soon as he saw Mark. The Penetrator pitched the suitcase in the backseat and got in the car. They were half a block away from the hotel tooling down Kuhio Avenue when they heard the police sirens. These Honolulu Police Department boys had a good response time on this one, Mark decided.

Uchi looked at Mark. "So?"

"Only two of them, one in the stairwell and one inside the room. I tied them up and left them with their silenced .45 for the police. They'll be in stir for two to five without any pain."

136

"And we hope they don't have anybody following us this time."

"Yeah, right. Look, Uchi, this is the end of the line. People are getting killed, and they're playing for keeps. I can't ask you to be part of this. No, that's not right. I won't *allow you* to be part of this."

Uchi gripped the wheel harder as he drove. He was checking behind to be sure no one was tailing them.

"Look, Uchi. You took your share of chances in 'Nam and somehow you came out of it alive. We owe you, the whole damn country owes you, and you're going to collect, so I don't want to see you shot up by some sex-crazy pornographers. This one is winding down now and you've done a good job for me. Let's have one last drink and talk about 'Nam and then we'll call it square."

Uchi pulled to the curb. "Hey, no way, man. I signed on for the whole tour of duty and I'm not quitting in midstream. What's with you? We went through things a thousand times more rugged than this. Hell, nobody has even *tried* to shoot at me yet. This is just a lazy walk in the morning sun. Remember that one in Lang Doc? We had three dead out of our team of seven, remember that? We didn't fold our tents and move into sick bay, did we?"

Mark tensed. "Uchi, how damn long do you think your luck is going to hold? The next slug that comes your way might nail you right between those slanted little beady eyes of yours and you'll say sayonara for the last time. No way! I'm making up the patrol roster, buddy, and you're not on it."

Uchi snorted. "One question. If my luck is about to run out, what about you? Haven't you been in this line of work for the last ten or eleven years? Why do you

137

think your luck is so much better than mine." He shrugged. "Hell, it's nothing to me. Just the seventh job I've fucked up on in the past three years. Hell, don't worry about me. What are buddies for anyway? You don't want me around, I can take a hint when it's a slap in the face. Let's have that one last drink. Then if I've got enough loot, I'll find some sexy broad in a cathouse and tell her my troubles."

Mark was grim as they went into a little bar. Uchi knew the barkeep, and they sat in a booth and lifted two, talking about 'Nam and the army in general, how it had given them a real fling, a chance that most men never have—to play war with real bullets.

"War is man's greatest adventure, did you know that?" Uchi asked. "It's the king of all the games ever invented. Man against man, the greatest sport in the universe. General Patton said something like that. His idea was: War is brutal, terrible, unthinkable, so amoral and outrageous that no thinking man could condone it—but, Goddamn, *I love it!*"

Mark nodded and drank. He wasn't sure about Uchi's attitude. He was taking this all too calmly. He knew he had hurt Uchi with the rebuff, but it was a lot better than staring down at his blood-covered, newly dead body.

They both had one more drink, then stood. Mark shook Uchi's hand, paid him nine hundred dollars (which Uchi protested, but at last took).

"Don't forget, you'll be hearing from Washington," Mark said. "I'm not going to let the army get away with messing around with my buddy, Uchi Takayama."

The small Japanese man nodded grimly, turned and marched away. Mark sighed. It was probably the last time he would ever see his wartime buddy, his true friend.

138

CHAPTER 14

A Shooting Session

Preacher Mann was furious as he glared at Kim Soong, his Korean business manager and silent partner.

"What do you mean your hit squad missed the Penetrator? How could it? One man was inside his room and one in the hall. How could two of them miss him?"

"The true serpent has many false heads, perhaps the men shot one of the false heads. I have no details, sir, only the fact that two of our best men are being held by the Honolulu police with their silenced weapon. No bail has been set yet on the felony; as I understand it the police found both men bound in the room's bathtub, and they are also being charged with the death of the printer."

"At least the printer was eliminated. You did something right for a change." He sat staring at the Japanese prints on the wall, trying to let their peace and tranquility relax him. He had the prints changed each week. "Drisana. Has she had time to settle herself? If she has,

139

I would like a few words with her, to tie down any other problems this Penetrator may make for us."

"I'll go see, Mr. Mann."

It was a delicate situation, and Preacher understood that. The girl from the mainland was important in the organization, yet she had failed on a mission. He let some of his anger dissipate. Killing the Penetrator was not just a simple mission, and in one way he sympathized with her. When she came through the sliding panel of pine and rice paper, the rest of his anger vanished.

Drisa wore a Japanese formal white kimono with flowered obi around her waist. Her breasts were flattened by the costume, and touches of the traditional white makeup of the geisha adorned her face. Her own hair was covered by a black lacquered geisha wig.

He applauded as she took mincing little steps across the tatami, then dropped to her knees in front of him and bowed with her forehead on the mat three times.

"Honorable *Papasan*, this unworthy one has come to pay homage at your feet."

"Oh, yes, I like it, Drisa. The kimono is perfect. It makes you look almost Japanese." He lifted her to her feet and motioned for her to sit on the floor pillows.

"Sorry about goofing on that Penetrator cat. He was good and so quick."

Preacher waved away her problem. "So you missed him, so what? We've got a dozen men out after him right now. A drink? Some tea, a little sake?"

She shook her head. "I'd rather have a bourbon on the rocks, a big one. Oh, hell just bring a bottle and a bucket of ice."

Preacher Mann chuckled. It had been some time since he had seen this remarkable girl, but she hadn't changed.

140

"Shit, I'm sorry about missing that damned Penetrator. I wasn't sure about him for a long time. Then when I decided it had to be him, whammo, he exploded like a madman. So help me, Preacher, I've never seen anybody move that fast or do so much in such a short time."

"Was he good in bed, Drisa?"

"Magnificent!" She smiled, then bowed low. "But not nearly as overpoweringly remarkable as you, oh wise *Papasan*."

Preacher's large brown eyes glistened as he watched her, small spots of perspiration beaded on his forehead; then he grinned, showing off his beautifully capped teeth. "I'll get to you just as soon as I can work you into my schedule," he said and laughed. "Oh, yes, and that will be soon. First some business."

He called in Kim Soong and told the Korean to double the guards on all installations, the house, the printing area, shipping, everywhere. To post a notice that a reward of $10,000 was waiting for the man who killed the Penetrator. Then he turned to the girl who had just splashed virgin bourbon over new rocks.

"We have a cover picture being shot. Would you like to come down and watch? It could be interesting."

"If there's a naked man involved, you're on," she said.

He took her hand, but she insisted on walking three paces behind him as any good Japanese woman should. Preacher Mann beamed.

The photo studio was on the first floor near the back. The room had no windows, and two pipes bristling with spotlights and other professional lighting gear hung near the ten foot ceiling.

A nude black man stood in the middle of the room in front of a backdrop on a roll of paper eight feet wide. It

141

showed a gentle spring season in New England, with newly leafing trees. A man on a stepladder was adjusting a spot on the man's face. The black was tall, slender, with powerful upper body and arms, showing a lot of weight training.

"Looking good, Wes," Preacher said to the black man.

"Thanks, Mr. Mann. This isn't my usual line of work."

"It sure should be," Drisa said. "You have a beautiful body, long and lean and sexy. Especially that part there in the middle."

Everyone laughed.

"Don't get him excited, Drisa, you'll spoil the shot."

A fully clothed assistant brought in two girls. They were both naked, about nine, with small breasts just beginning to swell. One of them was a delicate Chinese girl, with waist-length black hair. The second was a starkly pale white girl, with hair that had not turned yet from its youthful white-blonde. Her hair was cut short and shaped closely around her head. Both the young girls were tense, frightened, their faces frozen into solemn masks.

Preacher moved forward, helped position the girls, talking quietly to them, reassuring them. He put them first one way, then another on the bales of hay in the foreground, his big hands touching all over their bodies. Sweat beaded his forehead, and when he came back to Drisa after posing them, he was breathing faster than normal. Preacher glanced at Drisa, who noticed his excitement.

"God but they get to me," he told her quietly. "They're so pure, so perfect."

"And you'd like to hump them both at once right now, wouldn't you?"

142

He nodded, caught her hand, waved at the photographer, a sleek Chinese-Hawaiian girl, and went out the door. Preacher walked directly across the hall and opened a door and looked in. The office with a shag carpet on the floor was empty. He pulled Drisa inside, locked the door, and kissed her hard on her mouth. Then he spun her around and when she stopped, he slapped her gently on the cheek.

Her eyes flared a moment in anger, then she brightened in realization and she slapped him on the cheek. He slapped her again, harder, and she returned the blow. Now both were smiling. The next time he slapped her he pulled at her obi, loosening it. She slapped him on the arm, then grabbed the top of his shirt, jerking it quickly downward, popping half the buttons, slipping the others.

Preacher Mann laughed and shrugged out of the shirt, then hit her breasts with his open hand and she moaned softly. Preacher felt his excitement rising as the battle continued, and blows and clothes flew in all directions. He knew how it would end and he began to hum a little song as the girl hit him again.

An hour later Preacher put on his clothes and came out of the office, ducked into the studio and talked briefly with the photographer. She had taken ten different poses with the three, and ten shots of each pose. There should be ten or fifteen excellent pictures for him to choose from. He nodded and left, making a quick check on security.

First Preacher phoned, checking with the guards. Yes, there were double guards at the gate, along the fence, in the printing plant, and at the shipping point.

Preacher Mann sat at the communications room security board and watched it for a moment, then turned it back to the regular man. He saw nothing, but he knew the Penetrator was around *somewhere*, and he didn't want any slipups this time. There was no allowance for any disruption of the set schedules. The Penetrator must be killed as quickly as possible.

He had thought of sending Drisa out to look for the man. But that would be futile. The Penetrator would make it a point now not to go to any of the places he had been with her. It would be only a lucky chance if she saw him. No, he'd let his guards do that work—they were trained for it, and the man must be caught. The Penetrator must be killed or he would keep them all in constant danger. Preacher went back to the communication room and told the guards to spread the word: the price on the Penetrator had just gone up.

Now the man who brought in the Penetrator dead or alive would get a $50,000 cash bonus!

Mark drove around for almost ten minutes after he had left Uchi, before he was sure no one had followed him. Then he parked. He was in the nearest thing that Honolulu had to a downtown skid row. There were a few older bars, some boarded-up stores, one gutted by fire, and a closed up two-story, ancient hotel. Pawnshops dotted each block. Mark went into the nearest one and looked around. You could buy a little bit of anything in there; they must have a shotgun around somewhere. At the counter he found a young, bearded kid with blond hair reading a *Playboy* magazine.

"Yeah?"

"I want a shotgun, twelve gauge. An automatic that is unplugged or that I can unplug."

"Sure and I want a million dollars by Thursday. You nuts? You think I'm gonna risk ten years in the pen for selling an illegal weapon? And you a total stranger.

Sure, Mack, you must be smoking something good this morning."

"Come on, I need a piece, or a scatter-gun. I can pay extra."

"Yep, bet you're a Gestapo undercover jerk from the Bureau of Alcohol, Tobacco and Firearms. We get you guys in here testing us all the time."

"I'm not; I'm from the mainland and I need a shot-gun."

"Takes a three-day wait, Mack, and a police permit after a copper investigation. You get them, and I'll sell you any weapon I got in stock. And they're all legal."

"Thanks, cousin, you're all heart."

"Right, Mack, and I'm still on the outside, don't knock it."

Mark left grinning, he had to check the easy way. Now he worked the tough way, bumping into rough-looking characters in the area hoping to find someone who knew someone. Nothing. He spent another fast fifteen minutes trying to remember any illegal arms dealers he knew in the Islands. On the coast it was easier. At last he gave up and found a phone booth. He stared at the phone book instructions for a moment, then direct-dialed Portland, Oregon, using a long-remembered number and waited for the interrupt operator. It cost less than two dollars for three minutes, which he paid, then listened to the phone ring.

"Yeah?"

"Blackie, this is the Injun, remember me?"

"Hell, yes, you been a good customer, time to time."

"I'm across the lake in Hawaii, Blackie. I need some goods, but I've got no name. Can you help me?"

"How do I know you're really Injun?"

"You don't know my voice? How about this." Mark rattled off a long sentence in Cheyenne questioning the

quality of Blackie's breath and the state of his under-
wear. Blackie laughed for half a minute, replied in
equally unfriendly terms in the same language and then
went back to English.

"Hell, that's got to be you, Injun. I can't vouch for
this guy, but it's the first contact I ever had over there
and I guess it's good. Nobody complained."

He gave Mark a name and an address, and they said
good-bye, their business over. Mark stared at the address. It was out by Kailua somewhere. He would go
over the Pali Highway to the other side of the island.

Mark fished out his change and made another call.

"Junko? I'm Indian. I just had a talk with a man you
know, Blackie, in Portland. He says nice things about
you and that you can help me find some goods I need."

"Blackie? Oh, yeah, the guy on the mainland, Portland, Oregon. Yeah, I remember him. You need a good
batch of goods?"

"Three- maybe four-thousand-dollars worth depending what looks good."

"We ain't no supermarket, we're on order. Tell you
what. I'll make a call to Blackie, kind of double-check
like we always do. Got to protect the old backside. If
you're gonna be out this way about 2:00 this afternoon,
I'll sure be home and looking for you."

Mark said fine and hung up. He would have to leave
soon to get there in time. On the way he bought a
bunch of short, fat local bananas and ate half of them.
They tasted sweeter than the South American types he
was used to.

He found the address up a narrow dirt track through
incredibly green vegetation where you could look out
for miles on white surf just beyond a green carpet.
Mark parked as a huge Hawaiian man came around a
run-down shed.

"I'll talk, Injun. Talked to Blackie. He's says you're OK."

Mark sat on the Pinto's front fender as the big man waddled up. He was well over three hundred pounds and under five ten.

"You're looking?"

"True, I'm in need. You know Brownie in Seattle, and a little Jap in Los Angeles?"

"That little Jap got himself blown to hell."

"True, and half his stock with him. The way to go."

"That don't happen here, we're careful."

Mark nodded. "I'm hep. I'm also in need. Four fraggers, twenty quarter-pound blocks of C-4, an M-14 and six magazines filled, and a batch of detonator timers. About six WP grenades might come in handy, too. An automatic shotgun and twenty rounds of double-ought buck."

"You starting your own war?"

"Just against one badass who's got it coming. I'm not out to hurt anyone else, especially you."

"Hell, I don't care who you splatter around the Islands, just don't let anything be traced back to me. All I can give you is another name, another address."

Mark played the game. He had played it before, check and countercheck. He took the address and found it. They told him to go to another location. That's where the goods would be. He was parked near a beach with white crested waves crashing a hundred yards away. There wasn't a soul within a mile of him.

Then a car swirled up, two beach bums with boards got out and positioned themselves on each side of the entrance to the little turnoff. Each beachboy had an M-14 hidden behind his board.

The old Plymouth wheezed up and a small Jap-

147

anese man got out and smiled. He had brought everything but the M-14.

"Sorry, we're too short on the M-14's to sell them. We rent them out sometimes, but we figured you wouldn't want to bring one back. Instead we threw in twenty more rounds of double-ought buck for the shotgun and four extra WP grenades."

The price had been $4,000. Mark chopped off $500 for the M-14 and paid them $3,500 from his money belt. He usually carried ten thousand in it for emergencies.

"I'll give you ten minutes to get out of here," Mark said. The small man grinned, picked up his two surfers, and roared down the highway. Mark closed the trunk of his Pinto and watched the waves for a while.

He checked the road both ways and turned back toward the big city, but instead of cutting overland, he took the longer beach route. The road wound past Waimanalo and Sea Life Park, then around Hanauma Bay and Diamond Head before coming into the city. It was an interesting drive and Mark enjoyed it. He didn't have anything to do until it got dark, so Mark parked near Kapiolani Park and stretched out in the shade for a nap. He watched the beach and saw the joggers sweating past. At 7:00 he ate a dinner of clams, scallops, and a rare steak. Then he was back in the Pinto driving again, moving toward the Honolulu hills and the target for tonight.

CHAPTER 15

Printer's Devil Pies a Press

Mark had ordered his ordinance packed neatly in the kind of saddlebag that a newsboy carries papers in. It fit over his head, with big pouches in front and back which held the explosives, grenades, and shells. He would tie it down so it wouldn't hamper his movement.

Mark drove within a block of the warehouse they had found with the TV surveillance system and got out, taking the weapons pack with him. He was curious about the warehouse. It had to be some kind of an operation that was illegal. It had been listed by the printer- supply house as a place that had ordered materials and parts for a big press. It still could be tied in with the Preacher, and he wasn't passing up on any leads he had. If the place were benign, he would have risked little and lost nothing but a night's work. He would know quickly if this were part of the Preacher's empire. If so there would be some live guards on it now that the Preacher knew the Penetrator was in town.

Mark came up from the shielded side of the building,

149

checked the front, but saw no guards. He went into the shadows along the fence and used foot-long wire cutters to snip an eighteen-inch-high slice straight up from the ground on the cyclone fencing. The Penetrator cut the bottom strand of wire, then pulled up the flap of fence and was about to worm his way through when a voice behind him whispered.

"Where the hell you been, Sarge? I been waiting here for two hours!"

Mark whirled but even as he did he recognized Uchi Takayama's voice.

"Now, Sarge, none of your bullshit about my not playing the game. I knew you were trying to kiss me off so I wouldn't get hurt. Hell, what's there to hurt? This sounds like more fun than I've had in five years. And face it, you couldn't make this patrol without me. There are two guards just around the corner. They came out after you went by. I don't think they saw you, but they might have."

Mark reached out and grabbed Uchi's hand. It was what Uchi wanted, so why not? He nodded and worked his way under the fence. Uchi followed, then bent the flap of wire mesh back in place.

Mark pointed and they crawled to the side of the warehouse fifteen feet away, then stood. Mark handed Uchi the shotgun, two fraggers, and four of the white phosphorous grenades.

"Thanks, I don't feel quite so naked now. This scatter-gun is loaded, I'd guess?"

"Right, five rounds of double-ought buck. Cocked and locked."

Mark peered around the corner of the building and pulled back at once. He took Ava from his belt, the plastic dart gun that never had any trouble with customs or airline metal detectors. The customs people figured it was a toy, and the metal detectors saw only two small metal parts including the CO_2 propellant cartridge.

There was no time to explain the weapon to Uchi. Mark let the guard get almost to the corner, then he fired a dart. The soft hissing sound came quietly as the dart punctured the guard's thin uniform shirt and injected the combination of M-99 tranquilizer and sodium pentothal into the guard's tissue. Also in the mixture was an ingenious toxin that caused the voluntary muscles to go into spasms within a tenth of a second after the fluid hit the nerve tissue.

The guard had no time to cry out, no time to fire his weapon. He only groaned softly, then his arms and legs began spasming and he fell to the ground shaking and shivering for fifteen seconds when the tranquilizer took over and put him to sleep for fifteen minutes.

The second guard looked up from his post near the front door and saw his buddy go down.

"Hey, Loi, what the hell happened?" The second guard yelled it as he came running, his pistol out, eyes searching. Mark let him stop and bend over his partner before he shot him in the shoulder and watched him fall, twitching into slumberland.

"What the hell is that thing?" Uchi asked over Mark's shoulder.

"Tranquilizer," Mark said. He tossed Uchi plastic riot cuffs. "Cinch these on their ankles, I'll get their wrists. Then we drag them out of the way. They probably turned off the TV monitors while the live guards are on duty."

The door was locked, but keys from one of the guards provided entrance. Mark found no alarm and the TV cameras were off. He used a flashlight he had brought. Uchi had a light too, and quickly they discov-

151

ered that the place was a shipping point. It had a truck dock and on it were dozens of boxes of *Life Child*, posters and boxes of pedophilic glossy photos. It was definitely the Preacher connection. They had found part of the operation.

"So this is where they ship from," Uchi said. "Where the hell is the press? It sure ain't here."

They toured the rest of the warehouse, found a truck, a full-sized rig with a plain panel body on back, the way Larston Ohura had described. Under the hood were two long racks of heavy-duty truck batteries. It was an electric-powered truck.

They kept looking. Near the back of the big warehouse was a door. Mark stared at it and frowned.

"A big truck-sized door back here. Why?"

Uchi ran to the side of the door, studied it a minute, then snapped a switch, pushed a red button, and the truck door rolled silently back on oiled ball bearings revealing a huge, gaping black hole.

Uchi shone his light into the area, and so did Mark. Uchi let out a yelp of surprise.

"Hey, Mark, this is a lava tube. They are rare anywhere on earth."

"Looks like a tunnel big enough to drive that truck through."

"It is! It's fifteen feet in diameter! A lava tube is a tunnel that was formed by pahoehoe lavae. The surrounding lava on top and bottom and the sides has cooled and hardened, but the center here where we're standing was still boiling and bubbling, a liquid, and it flowed out and left this opening, a lava tube. I bet not many people know that this one is here."

"Preacher Mann knows it. Look at the tire tracks. That truck down there has been driving in and out of the tube."

"You're right. So let's see where it goes."

"We will, but first let's see how big a bonfire we can start in all that trash and rubbish down there."

Mark and Uchi went back to the stacks and cartons and jumbled some of the cartons so they would burn better, then threw white phosphorus grenades into the stack. The grenades exploded almost at once, raining furiously burning splatters of phosphorus onto everything. The phosphorus burned holes through boxes and cartons, setting the contents on fire. The fire would go through the roof quickly and that would bring a lot of attention.

"Let's get out of here," Mark said. They worked into the lava tube, using their lights. The floor was smooth, and Mark saw that it wasn't lava, it had been black-topped.

"Where the hell does this come out?" Uchi asked.

Mark shook his head. "My best bet is that it connects to another building where the books are printed. Then they are trucked underground over here for shipping. Aren't we going uphill?"

They were. The grade increased again and, after they had moved fifty yards, a small white light glowed along the side of the tunnel. They approached it carefully, but it was not a signal light of any kind. They passed it and moved ahead faster.

Mark heard a buzzing on his wrist. He looked down and saw the glow and showed it to Uchi.

"A sensitive wide-band receiver. It means we've tripped some sensors and a radio signal has been broadcast from along here somewhere. I'm not sure how far a radio signal would get through this lava, but some electronic fence has been tripped."

"So now we watch our ass, right?" Uchi snapped the safety off the shotgun and moved forward silently. They

153

went faster now, at a slow trot. There were more occa-
sional lights, and Mark tried to figure out how far they
had come. A half-mile? The tube turned and twisted
but there was always enough room for the big truck to
get through. Mark guessed it was still about fifteen feet
in diameter. Occasionally there would be a side tube but
these were short.

Mark outlined the battle plan. "We don't know what
we'll find up here, but if it is the press operation, we
blow it up first: that's the priority. They can do little
without it. We've got the C-4 and detonators—you
know how they work, you've used enough. Then we
disrupt anything else we can. But the workers are not
enemies. The only people we shoot at are the ones who
shoot at us first. Those will be the hard core, the goats,
the ones loyal to the whole underworld operation who
have sold out to Preacher Mann."

They passed more low-level lights and, after what
Mark guessed had been another half-mile upgrade, the
tube leveled out and they could see more lights ahead.
They moved along the sides of the tunnel and too late
Mark saw his body cross an electric-eye beam of light.
Suddenly two high-powered floodlights snapped on,
making the tunnel as bright as afternoon. They saw six
small electric golf cart rigs and two trucks parked in the
tunnel. Uchi blasted one of the floodlights with the
shotgun and Mark put two .45 slugs into the other. The
roar of the shotgun in the tunnel was deafening. They
lay on the dark floor watching, waiting. But there was
no return fire, no shouts of alarm, no running feet.

Mark motioned and they got up and ran for the end
of the tunnel they could see fifty yards ahead. At the
opening they paused and stayed in the shadows as they
looked out at a brilliantly lighted area.

Both men stared in surprise. They had found a huge

cavern. It was more than one hundred feet high and must have been several blocks long—one gigantic cave in the Honolulu hills. Inside they could see the myriad of lights, and the first of several all-aluminum warehouse buildings. A man rushed toward them now with a handgun spitting lead. Mark fired two rounds from his .45 and the man went down.

The two men charged ahead running hard for the edge of the building twenty yards away. Mark jerked open a door and they bolted inside, weapons ready.

It was a printing plant, complete with a huge press that stood twenty feet high and four times that long. Large rolls of paper stood on end, and stacks of magazines were on tables; boxes and shipping gear stood nearby. Mark looked for employees, guards, but saw no one. He nodded at one end of the press and gave Uchi some of the C-4.

"Use three packages, set the detonators for fifteen minutes," Mark said. They got to work and quickly the charges were placed in the big press in vital areas. They ran to the door at the far end of the two-hundred-foot-long building and opened the door carefully. Outside there was a paved street. They saw no one. Thirty yards ahead sat the next warehouse. They heard voices now, but saw no one. They rushed across the void, under the now too brilliant lights, and charged through the door into the second building.

A fifty-year-old Chinese man had just inserted a key in his night watchman's control box when they came in and almost bumped into him.

He took one look at the shotgun and held up his hands. He was nearly bald but had chin whiskers and a mustache.

"Don't shoot!" he said.

Uchi grinned. "Old grandfather, we won't hurt you.

Is this building the bindery? Do they put the books and magazines together here?"

The man nodded.

"Let's use the Willy Peter," Mark said. "You keep the guard with you. We'll take him with us. You go down about halfway, find two good spots and throw in two WP's. Then get out the far door. I'll use two on this end, and meet you outside. Let's move it, we don't have much time before that C-4 goes off. The whole top of this place might cave in when they blow."

Mark waited until he saw Uchi throw his first WP, then Mark tossed one into a jumble of glue pots, half collated pages and a big folding machine. It would go up like a torch.

He put the second WP grenade into shipping boxes and more stores at the far end of the warehouse, watched the flames start, and got out the door. Uchi came out at the other end and Mark ran to meet him. When he met them he motioned to the guard.

"What's in the next building?" Mark asked.

"Offices, photo studios, photo labs, more offices. Who are you guys?"

"Don't worry about it," Mark said. "Just show us the closest door into the next building."

The man ran in front of them toward the aluminum structure. Two men jumped from a small guardhouse before they got there and called on the trio to halt. Uchi sent a scattering of double-ought buckshot over their heads and they returned the fire but missed, then charged back inside the guard shack as Uchi banged through the door into the next building. They set the C-4 for five minutes and left two squares of it behind, then threw in another WP grenade each and found the far exit door.

Mark pushed it open and stepped back. Six slugs

slammed through the door from an automatic weapon.

"What's in the other buildings?" Mark asked the Chinese.

"Next one is storage. Last one is barracks for workers, about twenty there, and ten guards," he said, looking frightened.

Mark touched his shoulder. "You get down there and sound an alarm, pull a fire alarm or something and get those people out of there. Is there a way to the surface?"

"Yes, stairs about fifty yards on up the street."

"Get those people up the stairs, this whole cave is going to blow up any minute. Take a back door out of here if there is one."

The Chinese nodded and ran along a wall to the other side of the building. Uchi pushed the shotgun out the door and let go with a blast, then jammed new rounds into the weapon to keep it filled. Keeping out of the line of fire, Mark swung one of the doors inward and left it open. No fire came. He looked around the door, saw two curious guards thirty yards away.

Mark fired over their heads and they fired back, but missed as they ran back to a small building and fired from around it. Mark and Uchi charged out the door, dodging from side to side, firing at the guards as they ran to the next big building. They could smell smoke behind them now.

"We've got about three minutes," Mark said. They had almost reached the next doorway when two guards ran down steps to the right and opened fire with automatic weapons. Lead zipped and whipped around the two invaders but didn't make contact.

Both dove behind a stack of lumber and peered around it. The guards were both black and came down the stairs that led upward. They crouched near the structure. Mark judged the distance and fired twice with his .45. The second round picked off one of the guards who'd been not quite out of sight. The other one dragged his partner out of danger.

"Keep them pinned down," Mark yelled. He darted into the next-to-last warehouse. It was a jumble of stores, construction material, and supplies. Mark threw two fragmentation grenades into the stores, then set a C-4 explosive quarter-pounder for three minutes and tossed it into the mess. He ran outside and dove for the stack of lumber.

That's when the door of the last building burst open and five men ran for the steps, pulling on clothes as they came, buttoning up, and looking at the smoke in front of them with fear and wonder.

Shortly two women came, then five more persons, and all congregated at the steps. The guards seemed to be arguing with them; then one of the men drew a knife and thrust it at the guard and the surge of people pushed past the injured man and rushed up the steps.

Mark and Uchi knew that was their one way out, to follow the workers. Before they could run into the dozen or so people at the steps, two deep-seated roaring explosions came from far down the cavern. Smoke billowed, dust and dirt showered down from the million-year-old roof of the cave. Now smoke and dust filled the air, and they coughed as they ran for the stairs.

Another dozen men and women charged from the far barracks and pushed around Mark and Uchi as they began moving up the steps. No more guards could come down the stairs as the frightened group of people hurried upward.

There were four levels of steps bending back on themselves, with about forty steps in each group. Mark wondered what they would find on top. The mass of bodies ahead of them slowed. No one looked at their clothes, or the shoulder bags Mark still wore. One or two glanced at the shotgun, but were more worried about the fire below.

At the top more lights showed, and the group slowed again. Mark could see over most of the people, and he observed that they were coming out in a metal building in a glare of lights. Some of the people were rushing out a far door.

Then Mark saw why the line had slowed. Two men with submachine guns at the ready were checking each worker as he or she came out. Both men with the guns were black, and each one had to be watching carefully for the Penetrator!

CHAPTER 16

A Preacher in the Hand Is Worth . . .

Mark knew he couldn't shoot in the crowded room. He signaled the idea to Uchi and they split, one going on each side of the twin line and, on a lifted-eyebrow signal they had used dozens of times before, both surged past others standing in front of them, bodies blocking the big black men holding the submachine guns and knocking them sprawling among a mass of arms and legs of bystanders. Then Mark and Uchi darted through the doorway and into a lighted yard where they found twenty or thirty people standing around watching the opening, and waiting.

Mark and Uchi walked through the group, then dodged behind more persons and ran at flank speed into the darkness just beyond. Behind them they heard the guards screaming. The submachine-gun carriers charged through the small metal shed door at the head of the stars, glowering.

"Those men who ran out of here. Where did they go?" one guard screamed. Somebody pointed the way they had vanished. Another man pointed in the opposite direction. The guards cursed and split, each going into the darkness in a different direction.

Mark waited near the edge of the blackness. He stood by a Japanese fountain next to an eight-foot-tall tree fern. The guard who came his way knew the path. He ran along at full speed, probably planning to stop a short distance into the darkness and listen. Mark watched him come as he surged out of the light. As he came directly opposite where Mark stood, the Penetrator swung his arm to meet the black man.

The runner's own speed plus Mark's arm motion clotheslined the guard in the best National Football League tradition. Mark's arm barely grazed the man's chin, slid under it and crashed into his throat with such force it broke the man's neck, and he crumpled to the ground without a sound.

Uchi had waited a dozen feet beyond, and now he ran back, picked up the MP-40 submachine gun from the dying black man and he and Mark ran into the darkness and upward on the slope.

"This is the place I was telling you about," Uchi said when they stopped. "This is that showplace, that Japanese mansion. Look at it!"

The big house spread out below them, three stories high with a large garden and fishponds behind it, small Oriental bridges, shrines, and ornamental plantings, and carefully tended shrubs and small trees. It could have been in Tokyo.

"Isn't this something! It's beautiful. So Preacher Mann bought this place and somehow discovered the cavern down below and the lava tube. . . ."

"Look," Mark said. Below, the workers were being pushed into groups and marched down the road, away from the mansion. Evidently they would go to other

161

quarters. Just then there was a loud sound and a rush of smoke came pouring from the small metal building over the stairway to the cavern.

"Seems like some of our charges are going off below," Mark said. "We've taken care of the printing plant; now we have to chop off the head of this monster, Preacher Mann himself."

"In the big house?" Uchi asked.

"Right, down there in the mansion."

Far away they heard sirens, fire sirens. That would be the firemen going to the warehouse, Mark decided. He studied the big structure below, trying to figure the best way to assault it.

Then he spotted a dozen men, all armed with submachine guns, come out of the house, each take a sector and fan out into the darkness. They were after Mark and Uchi.

Another explosion rocked the ground and more smoke gushed from the small building over the stairs. Suddenly the lights in the yard snapped off, with only those left on in the house.

Uchi crawled up beside Mark. "You go inside. I'll keep our friends occupied out here. Here comes one. Keep cool and lay low."

Uchi pulled the narrow leather belt from his waist and stood beside an ornamental pine tree. As the hunter with the machine gun came closer, he worked his way around the four-foot-thick pine on one side. Uchi edged around it on the other side staying out of his sight. Once behind the guard, Uchi surged forward, looped the belt over the man's head and jerked it tight, strangling him. He let the man sag against the belt increasing the pressure until the man went limp. When Uchi was sure the man was dead he dropped him to the

162

ground, picked up his submachine gun and gave it to Mark.

"Give me that bag of goodies. Let me keep them busy out here and you can go inside and have your fun." Uchi said. Mark passed the bag with the remaining explosives and grenades to Uchi, and watched the slight little Japanese warrior fade down a white seashell path.

Mark held the familiar MP-40 machine gun, made sure it was charged and the safety was off. Then he moved down another path toward the house. He chose a back room for his entrance. For a moment he thought of wading across a shallow fishpond to get in on an unprotected balcony almost at the water's surface. But he decided not to, edged around the water on a narrow dike, and leaped the last four feet to another balcony on the other side. He turned abruptly as he heard a five-round burst from one of the guns in back of him chatter into the night. But the slugs did not come toward him. There was no answering fire. He heard a scream, then silence. Mark knew the action had come from Uchi. It was his old "keep them guessing" tactic they had used so well before.

Mark paused on the edge of the narrow wooden balcony, looking at the sliding panels of pine covered with rice paper. It was traditional, but he guessed there would also be some modern sophisticated security devices as well.

Mark pulled the sliding panel back six inches, then paused. He heard nothing. He pushed the panel backward again another six inches. There was no reaction. Mark pulled off his belt and swung the heavy brass buckle inside the room through the opening. There was a flash of fire; he jerked the belt back, and in the dim

163

light could see how the brass buckle had been melted on one side by a powerful charge. The stabbing electrical beam seemed to come from a box on the left side of the panel. Receiver or sender, it didn't matter. Mark kicked it with his heavy-soled half-boot from the bottom, jolting it halfway off the wall. He heard a low whine which he hoped meant the unit was out of service. Mark swung the belt buckle through the opening again and there was no reaction. He stepped inside, the machine gun held at his side. He was in a bedroom area, with a Japanese floor bed and sand pillows.

Mark's night vision now let him see that there were no other intrusion devices in the room. He crossed, slid another door back six inches, and looked into the hall.

If the guard had been a better shot, Mark would have been dead. The intrusion malfunction must have registered on some alert board, and a small black man holding a .45 edged down the hallway looking for the right opening. When the panel moved, he fired, the slug missing Mark's head by inches.

Mark's MP-40 lifted a fraction of an inch and he fired a three-round burst that stitched three new buttonholes up the man's chest, slamming him against the wall where he slid to the floor, both hands over his chest. He died before Mark walked up the hall.

Mark ran along the hall now, heard a grenade go off outside the house and another machine gun chatter. He knew Uchi was playing his part in the game to the hilt.

Mark hurried toward the end of the hallway where he saw brighter lights and could hear excited voices. A panel opened just in front of him and an unsuspecting black man came into the hall. He saw Mark and lifted his hands silently. Mark's burp gun centered on the chest.

"Trun around slow, friend, or eat lead." The man turned slowly, anger and frustration on his face. Mark slammed the receiver of the weapon across the fuzzy black head and the man crumpled. The Penetrator jumped over the man and ran lightly to the end of the tatami mat-covered hallway.

A two-story section opened in front of him. Thirty feet across the room, Mark saw Preacher Mann towering over five or six excited women bunched in front of him. Everyone seemed to be shouting.

"Preacher Mann. Don't move. I've got a machine gun trained on your big gut. Move and I'll plaster you all over the tatami!"

Preacher Mann's big arm swung out and trapped one of the women in front of him and pulled her closer to his own bulk. It was Drisana.

"Go ahead, Penetrator. If you're good enough to miss them and hit me, blast away. These are innocent people here." Preacher laughed as Mark hesitated, then he dragged the girl backward, jumped into an elevator and, keeping her in front of him, closed the door. Mark guessed the elevator went upward.

Six others in the room began firing at Mark. He sent several rounds at them and charged for a curved stairway to his left. He was out of sight of the shooters in a few seconds, moving upward cautiously. Mark realized he was on his own now, in a strange place. He had no idea of the terrain and he knew that the Preacher had all the cards, all the troops.

Then from below he heard the familiar wail of a siren, and out a window saw two long, red fire engines rushing up the street toward the entrance to the big house and the smoke billowing below. There would be some friendly troops in the area soon.

A bullet splattered the highly lacquered wooden carved stair railing just behind him and slanted into the wall.

Mark jolted to one side, fired a burst from the machine gun, and ran on to the second landing, his eyes alert for any movement, any sign of the Preacher.

The second floor showed only a dozen more rooms opening off a long hall. If Preacher Mann went upward, he would probably go to the top floor, Mark decided. It was what Mark would do in the same situation.

He ran up the last flight of steps and came to a set of polished and varnished doors. There were no windows, and the doors swung, meeting in the center. Mark stayed behind the wall and pushed one of the doors with the muzzle of the weapon. The door creaked inward, then swung back. The rear swing was accented with three rounds from a heavy handgun firing from inside. Mark pushed the door again, but there was no reply. The next time he held it partly open with the muzzle of the MP-40 so he could look inside.

It was a thirty-foot-long lounge area, with Western furniture mixed with Oriental floor cushions. Windows along one side had been blocked out with delicately painted Japanese folding screens. He heard no movement, saw no one.

Then a long laugh came and Mark tensed. It was the Preacher. The sound seemed to come from all over the room, echoing and bouncing from place to place. It was amplified and must have come from a dozen speakers.

The laugh ended with a shrill line that faded away in the best doppler principle.

"Penetrator, catch me if you can. . . ."

Mark leaped into the room, but saw only what could be elevator doors at the far end. His weapons swung, covering the thirty-foot room, but there was no one there. It was empty. Low-key Japanese paintings adorned the walls, while the floor was highly polished wood. But Preacher Mann had escaped, somewhere.

Had he gone down the elevator? Why had he come up here on the elevator if he was going to go right back down? No, Mark guessed he was somewhere closer by, watching, perhaps watching expectantly. The Preacher wasn't through yet. Mark tensed, his finger on the MP-40, ready to fire that submachine gun at a microsecond's warning.

CHAPTER 17

Don't Feed the Hand That Bites

Mark stood only three feet into the room on a short tatami runner. He saw no place in the rectangular room where the big man and the girl could be hiding. Where were they? Had they used the elevator?

He started to run forward but stopped. The shining, lacquered floor glistened right in front of him, but he didn't put down his outstretched foot. The floor was too perfect, too shiny and smooth.

Mark pulled a quarter from his pocket and tossed it on the surface. Immediately the coin sputtered and bounced, then it melted into a small puddle of metal. The floor was electrified.

Mark sidestepped on the tatami to another stretch of the fabric-like rice straw mat and ran along its length to the elevator. He saw that the door had been blocked open with a chair. The elevator had not been used. Mark wheeled, expecting a murderous assault, but still found no one in the room. The screens, the painted movable screens at the far side of the room!

Mark ran past the elevator on the tatami to the screens and pushed the first aside. Drisa smiled up at him. She sat on a floor bed and had just pulled off her blouse. She grinned up mischievously.

"Lover! My very own *Penetrator!* Hey, you're just in time for the party, so come on in."

Mark bent and checked the pile of her clothes on the quilted blankets, but found no weapon. He quickly cinched riot cuffs on her wrists, then pushed her aside and ran to the next set of delicately painted screens. These showed a dragon belching fire over a set of white mountaintops.

Mark knocked the screens down.

A huge German shepherd attack-trained dog was already in midair leaping for Mark's throat. The MP-40 came up as Mark lashed out with the heavy receiver part of the weapon, catching the dog just under the chin in the upward slash, breaking the dog's jaw. The animal was jolted into unconsciousness, fell to one side, and lay still. Mark ran forward, the weapon now in both hands ready to fire.

Directly ahead he came to the wall that was flush with the area where he entered from the steps. There was a Western-type door with a knob. It opened inward. Mark reached for the knob, then changed his mind and kicked the door beside the knob with his boot, breaking the latch, swinging the door inward.

It was a hot tub, a Japanese bath with steaming sulfur water, small dip pans and brushes, a dozen white towels laid out, and a young Japanese girl bare to the waist bowing and ready to take care of his bathing needs. Mark stepped inside and looked around.

He frowned, but before he could spin around, the door he had kicked open, closed by itself and locked; then a thin, strong metal mesh dropped down from the

169

ceiling and locked in place on the floor. The Japanese girl scooted backward through a two-foot-high swinging panel and at the same time a mesh fell on that side of the room and locked in place.

The Preacher laughed.

"Welcome, Penetrator. This is a little surprise I've been saving for you. It's called my persuasion room. Ever heard of a real bloodbath? This is where you're going to have one. But it won't be quick. Oh, no. I have too many debts to collect from you for that. I have the whole Florida expedition and my cryogenic projects. You ruined me there. I had to start over. But luckily I had a little help."

Mark saw the speaker in the ceiling and sent three rounds into it from the machine gun. The noise was painful.

The voice laughed again. "Oh, I expected your violence. There are twelve speakers built into the room. If you want to, you can shoot them all out. Instead, why don't you worry about the problem at hand? You could take a hot tub bath before you die. Or perhaps you don't want to waste the time. But you will have plenty of time from now on, Penetrator. Death is for such a long time, why rush it?"

Mark realized that the hot water had all drained from the tub. It was empty. Now a gas hissed into the room. Mark wanted to fire at the vent but knew it would do no good.

"Don't worry, it isn't fatal," Preacher said. "Just some good old reliable tear gas. I want to hear you cry, Penetrator. Is that too much to ask after all you've done to me?"

The gas came faster. Mark reached for his special handkerchief, the one he took with him in every set of clothes he wore. It had enough chemicals built into it to

170

render most poison gases harmless. He folded it twice and put it over his nose, and breathed in the sweet pure air, but that wouldn't help his eyes.

Preacher laughed again.

"Now for a new surprise, for the soon-to-be-dead Penetrator. Watch my smoke. I call it my computer-programmed death machine. It all depends how lucky you are how long you can survive. Don't worry, one or two probably won't kill you. At least I hope not. That would spoil all of my fun."

From behind him Mark heard the sudden hissing of compressed air. He spun and saw small circles on the papered wall at the right side suddenly break open and four dartlike projectiles shoot toward him. Mark fell to the floor. The darts embedded in the wooden wall eight feet across the square room. The darts were six inches long, with two-inch bow-and-arrow hunting tips on them that would make a three-inch-wide slash if they hit his body.

"Curious fun, isn't it, Penetrator? I have no idea where the computer will launch the next darts. It's all automatic, and devised by an ingenious little Korean who is excellent at his work."

Another dart hissed through the air. This one came less then six inches off the floor and arched into the tatami mat before it reached the far wall.

The tear gas had stopped. A fan somewhere sucked out the gas but it had made Mark's eyes water. He wiped them dry as he looked at the darts. The solution was simple. He jumped into the three-foot-deep tub and crouched down. He was out of the range of the darts.

"Ah, my pressure gauges show that you are in the tub. Very ingenious, Mr. Penetrator. But look upward. What do you see?"

Mark looked up. There were dozens of small vials on

the ceiling and one of them broke and a liquid fell toward him. Only a small bit of it hit his wrist but it burned like a live coal. Mark spit on the spot trying to wash off the fluid.

"Yes, yes, I see you have felt some of it," Preacher said. "It's a beautiful combination of carbolic acid, electrolyte acid from a car battery, and good old phenol. Enjoy, Penetrator, enjoy."

Mark leaped from the tub as the ceiling erupted with dozens of drips of the burning acid.

Another firing of darts slanted through the air. He tried to listen for the tearing of the paper so he could judge where the darts were coming from. It was impossible.

Then he saw the solution. The towels! There were a dozen thick, dry, large bath-sized towels. He grabbed them and jumped to the wall with the darts. Quickly he unfolded five of the towels, used four of the spent darts from the other wall, and pounded them into the dart wall, holding up the towels. He used the butt of the machine gun as a hammer. The taut towels should be able to mute or stop the darts, especially so close to the source. He stood at one side and watched. Two darts fired behind the towels. One stopped, the other tore the towels loose from the wall.

Mark rushed back to the spot, put up three more towels over the thickness and pounded in more darts firmly around the edges. Another dart fired within the four-foot-high, three-foot-wide towel area. It did not penetrate.

Now was the time for acting. Mark crouched behind the towel and fired three rounds from the machine gun into the dart wall. Then he screamed,

"Preacher, let me out! Damnit, let me out of here. This is inhuman. Meet me face to face!"

172

Mark waited to see if the Preacher had pickup mikes in the torture room. He did.

"So, I've finally got to you, tough man. How does it feel to bleed, to hurt, to be in frustration and facing death? The darts will get you—there's no way you can deny them. You can't shoot them out. The electric power is so deep in the sides of the wall you can't get to it."

Mark picked up one of the spent darts and threw it at the chain mesh along the side walls. As he expected there was a flash as the charged wire sent out a shower of sparks and the metal dart danced and twisted as it fell down the chain.

"Ah, so. You tried the fence. Too bad. Did you burn your little fingers, Penetrator?"

More darts hissed.

"Don't worry, Penetrator. It won't be long now. The dart board is programmed to play with you for a while, then it will launch a wholesale attack and you will be riddled. Won't that be fun, Penetrator? You can't imagine how I'm enjoying all of this. Soon I'll come in and administer the coup de grâce. Now that will be the thrill of a lifetime for me."

Mark sent an answering five-round burst into the dart wall, and the Preacher laughed over the mike.

"Fight it, fight it! But you must realize there's no way you can win, Penetrator."

Mark pressed hard against the protective towels. He folded the last two and made a thicker cushion he put next to his side where he pressed against the towels. He waited.

More darts came, then in a whooshing blur, fifty or sixty darts slanted through the air at once. Mark felt four, then five darts struggle to get through the masses of fabric next to his body, but the cloth dulled and

173

stopped the weapons. Mark saw the darts fly and played his role. He screamed. Then he fired at the wall, and screamed again and dropped the machine gun on the floor, carefully so he could still reach it. He had rounds left in the thirty-round magazine.

"Penetrator, how are you feeling now?" There was a pause. "Penetrator?" Another pause. "Come on, Penetrator, speak to me and I'll let you go.

Mark picked up the weapon silently. His one fervent hope was that there was no visual window into the room, no TV monitor camera. He waited as the screen mesh on the door wall unlatched at the floor and rose silently into the ceiling. Then the door opened a small crack and Mark Hardin jerked the door inward, pulling Preacher Mann against the doorjamb, dazing him, sending him reeling backward.

Preacher saw Mark surge out of the doorway, uninjured, and he screamed and grabbed Drisana and pulled her in front of himself.

"Nice try, Preacher, but no rubber duck."

The big man had no gun with him, he moved backward along the low tables in the room. He was twenty feet away.

"Don't hurt me, Penetrator. I didn't hurt you none," Drisana said. "Don't blast both of us with that tommy gun just to kill him."

Mark ignored her. He wanted her alive, if possible, but Preacher would try to stop that.

When Preacher reached the table he bent down and came up with a stick of dynamite trailing a foot-long fuse. He laughed at Mark, and put the dynamite on Drisa's head.

"Go ahead, bad man. Shoot us now. The blast will take you with it." He flicked on a lighter and held it near the fuse. Mark looked at the dynamite in surprise.

It was sweating and actually wet with bulges in places. It was old and he was sure it was now terribly unstable.

"Go easy with that stuff," Mark said. "Can't you see it's so old and sweating that it could go off if you even bump it hard?"

"No more of your tricks, Penetrator. I've had enough of them for one day. You won't shoot because you know those chatter guns are notoriously inaccurate. And I'm going to light this bomb and hold it to the very last second, then toss it over there and let it blow you into mincemeat."

He lit the fuse. Mark wanted to try to shoot the big man, but Preacher was right. A slug might jolt off the slight line by a foot or more from the inaccurate little submachine gun. The fuse was lit and burning. Mark had only one bet left. When Preacher tried to throw the bomb, Mark would blast away with the SMG. Fire his last four rounds.

"Get ready to die, Penetrator. I've waited a long time for this." He held the bomb high for a moment, then put it against Drisa's stomach and walked her slowly toward Mark.

The Penetrator retreated, moving over near the windows where the heavier Western furniture sat. He might be able to slap the bomb out the window or even behind some furniture.

"No use running, you're a dead man," Preacher chortled.

Preacher lifted the bomb with one hand, then almost dropped it and quickly reached up with his other hand. When Drisa was free she spurted away from Preacher and ran the other way. Mark lifted the muzzle of the MP-40 and fired a four-round burst. The slugs traced a line up the Preacher's forearm and wrist and then one slug hit the unstable dynamite and the whole room seemed to explode in one giant fireball. Mark felt himself blown off his feet and rolled five yards along the floor before he stopped.

He sat up, trying to clear his head, trying to stop the pounding, roaring still in his ears. Most of the screens next to the windows had been blown over. Most of the windows were shattered. He saw Drisa stagger to her feet and then collapse in a chair. Where was Preacher?

Mark got unsteadily to his feet, found everything worked, and walked to where the bomb went off. It had been four feet from a window. On the floor near the shattered glass he found one of Preacher's black hands. A trail of blood smeared the window ledge and seemed to move downward.

Mark looked out the window and saw the big man lying on the edge of one of the fishponds three stories below. He was conscious. Preacher's left leg slid down the slippery bank and splashed in the water.

The Penetrator stared in surprise as the surface of the water around Preacher's leg erupted in a froth. Something in the water was attacking Preacher's leg. Mark could think only of the voracious, deadly South American piranha.

Preacher Mann screamed, a death cry of total defeat, of a misspent life, of a dream of debauchery that almost came true. Mark watched in surprise and horror as Preacher slid lower and lower on the moss-covered cement lip of the pool. Then his whole body fell into the churning pink frothy water and his head bobbed once, then vanished under the feeding frenzy of little fish. The foaming and splashing in the quickly red water would continue for almost five minutes before the surface became calm again.

When Mark turned away he found Drisa sitting in the same chair, one arm hanging uselessly at her side,

176

her eyes barely open. Shards of glass were embedded in her forehead and neck, and she bled profusely. She made no attempt to stop the blood.

As he turned toward her she lifted a .45 automatic and aimed it at him. She blinked several times, but still blood seeped into her eyes.

Mark no longer carried the machine gun, but he had his own .45 on his hip.

"I'm not going out that way," Drisa said. "Damn, it must have been his lovely little assassins, the piranha, right? He ended up the same way several of his enemies did."

Mark nodded. "It was the piranha."

"I'm not going out that way."

"You're not going out at all. I need you as a witness against this operation."

"It's over. It's blown. Can't you see that? The whole network is down, it may never be put together again. The league, the wholesalers, the distributors, the retailers, it's all over. I hear you even got my nana. It's over. All over, so I might as well take you with me."

Again with no more warning than that Drisana fired. The big .45 slug tore through Mark's left arm, high up, spinning him around. He fell backward, drawing his own weapon, rolled once and fired. He heard her gun firing twice more but the slugs missed. Mark's round took her through the forehead, just over the right eye, slamming her back in the soft chair, spinning the weapon from her lifeless hand.

As his shot sound died, Mark heard a bullhorn from the outside.

"All right, we've got this whole compound under control. Anyone in the house is under arrest. Come out now with your hands up."

Mark looked out a window and saw police below,

along with the firemen. He ran to the back of the house, opened a window and jumped down to a second-story roof. Only then did he realize how much his left arm hurt. The jolt of his landing on the roof almost made him cry out. He held the arm with his right hand, and worked across the roof. Above in the rocks he heard a machine gun rattle. Men from below ran that way. Mark looked over the eaves of the second story, found a downspout, and studied it. Yes, he could make it with one hand. He groaned as he went over the lip of the roof and caught the pipe, then slid down faster than he wanted to the first-floor roof fighting the pain from his left arm. Once on the roof he held his left arm tightly and jumped to the ground. He let out a soft moan when he landed jarring his arm. Then he struggled to his feet and ran into the darkness of the gardens above the fishponds. His arm throbbed, hurting more than anything he could remember for a long time.

Mark moved as silently as he could. He heard another chatter of a machine gun upward and to the left. He moved away from it to the right but high into the rocks and ledges and the greenness of the Hawaiian landscape. He knew there was no chain link fence up there. It was a hard climb. He fell once on his wounded arm and a wave of pain swept over him with a sharpness that surprised him.

Mark stuffed his arm in his shirt front to hold it as steady as he could and ran low. There was movement to his left but he couldn't worry about it. All he had to do now was fade away.

His arm throbbed and for a moment he concentrated on bringing on his *sho-tu-ca* powers of the Cheyenne Dog Soldier, but somehow the right words and phrases slipped away from him, and he couldn't remember them all, or get in the right state of mind.

178

He felt blood on his elbow. Mark stopped and checked the wound. It was bleeding much more than he thought. And now he realized it was bleeding too much, he was losing more blood than he should. Dizziness swept over him and he heard noise behind him, closer now. Slowly he turned, to lift the .45 from his belt, but he couldn't, it was so heavy. Then the form was on top of him, grabbing the gunhand, forcing it down.

Mark shook his head. Someone had slapped his face. He blinked and realized he had passed out. He blinked again, tried to get his eyes focusing. When things cleared he looked up to see an Oriental face staring down at him. The Cong! The damned Cong had captured him! He tried to lunge upward, but hands held him down. Then a voice came through that he knew.

"Sarge. Sarge, damnit, snap out of it. We got to get our asses out of here! Come on Mark, get things together!"

Mark Hardin grinned weakly, pushed back the mists and waves of pain and the infuriating weakness and staggered to his feet.

"Yeah, let's move, Uchi. You damned little Chopsticks, let's get out of here!"

EPILOGUE

Mark came out of the little cabin and stretched out in the folding director's chair by the rail in the soft Hawaiian sunshine. The twenty-four-foot motor cruiser rolled easily in the swells over the Tri-Mar Reef, where Uchi said there was some of the best rock cod fishing in the world.

Mark eyed the bottom rig for a moment and the six-foot heavy pole with the big four-0 reel, then picked up the six-hook ganglion and the one-pound lead sinker. His left arm twinged as he lifted the pole, then lowered the sinker over the rail and the bait hit the water. They were in twenty fathoms here. He lowered away until the sinker hit the reef, reeled it up two turns and waited. Uchi had baited the six hooks.

Uchi had been doing a lot of things for him lately. Uchi had pulled him out of the Preacher Mann estate and saved him from being arrested by the HPD. He had taken Mark to one of his uncles who was a doctor and who patched Mark's arm back together where the .45 slug had messed up the big artery. Uchi had saved his life—again.

The Hawaiian papers had been headlining the raid, the fire, and the caverns for a week now. The big cav-

180

ern and the long, huge lava tube had been found and were at once named state parks by the in-session legislature. Preacher had found the lava tube first as he dug a cave into the cliff through the back of his warehouse so he would have a safe place to hide things in case he was raided. The lava tube led to the cavern and he originated his plans to build his printing plant inside. Then he dug the stairwell to the surface, found out where it came to the top, and brought the land surrounding the new entrance.

Now the cavern would be a state park, in spite of what the big corporate owners of the land had in mind.

Mark felt a tug on his line and he jerked it sharply upward, hooking a cod he hoped, and let the line settle down, waiting for another visitor to one of the other baited hooks.

Preacher Mann was identified by his dental work when they pulled his skeleton from the pond. The piranha had left little more of him than the bones. The fish had been netted and transferred to a freshwater tank in a marine park where they were put on display, and feeding time became a big attraction for tourists and locals alike.

Mark had phoned Dan Griggs in Washington, gave him Uchi's service number and record, and demanded that Dan put through a disability claim for Uchi and to see that it was approved pronto. Dan had grudgingly let himself be bulldozed. He had already heard about the demise of Preacher Mann and the pedophilia literature production facility and distribution network. Also the International Pedophilia League was shattered. Mark had saved the Justice Department a million dollars in operational man-hours alone.

The biggest surprise was when Mark called Captain

181

Kelly Patterson of the Los Angeles Sheriff's Department. Kelly had responded to Mark's call with glee.

"Glad you got the bastard, but did you find out he was only the third in command? True. The whole thing was run by your favorite little old grandmother, Mrs. Martha Berstrom from right here in San Fernando. Remember her? You questioned her way back after we picked up a friend of hers. And guess who her kinfolk is? Right, your Drisana playmate was the number two head of the whole thing. She was a courier, problem-solver, order-giver, expert in publishing and marketing. She spent about half her time in the Islands. She didn't work for the movie man, Paul McMillen, in Hollywood. McMillen worked for her! She owned the studio, the whole shebang. She helped you fold the place with the hopes she could stop you down the line. Glad she missed."

Mark had been properly surprised, but ever since Drisana had mentioned her "nana" before she started shooting he had been trying to figure out her true place in the organization.

Mark tugged again and then again on the pole, and yelled for Uchi. His injured left arm couldn't hold the pole well enough to reel in the catch.

"Hey, Captain Uchi, come reel this batch in. I've got a ton of them on."

Uchi pushed the blue yachting cap back on his head, took the pole from Mark, and reeled up the line. Mark had caught three salmon grouper about six pounds each, a ten-pound ling cod, and one small bonito.

When Uchi had lifted the load over the rail, he stood there panting. "Isn't that enough?" he asked. "We've got fish to feed the Takayama clan for a month now."

Mark laughed and agreed. He went below and watched Uchi working on a marine watercolor painting.

Mark shook his head in mock disbelief. "You mean people actually have agreed to *pay* good money for that stuff?"

Uchi nodded. "So far, so good. I've sold twelve of my charcoal sketches, including some of the 'Nam ones. They aren't going for big bucks yet, but I'm working at it. What do you think of this one?"

Mark looked closer. The watercolor was Hawaiian, with lots of blues and greens. In the foreground at a dock was a fisherman standing beside a two-hundred-and-fifty-pound marlin hung from a pole. The fisherman was unmistakably Mark Hardin.

"I like it," Mark said. "Give you three hundred for it."

"Sold," Uchi said. "I thought you'd like it. Now let's see if we can scare up a mahi mahi or two on some trolling. It's time for you to tie into one of the big ones."

Mark took over the wheel as Uchi lifted the sea anchor. Smashed-up arm or no, he was determined to have another week in Hawaii with nothing to do but enjoy himself. He smiled, pushed in the throttle, and spun the boat around as he headed in the direction Uchi pointed out and throttled back to six knots, a good trolling speed.

by Lionel Derrick

THE PENETRATOR

More bestselling action/adventure from Pinnacle, America's #1 series publisher!

☐ 40-101-2 Target Is H #1	$1.25	☐ 40-258-9 Radiation Hit #20	$1.50
☐ 40-102-0 Blood on the Strip #2	$1.25	☐ 40-079-3 Supergun Mission #21	$1.25
☐ 40-422-0 Capitol Hell #3	$1.50	☐ 40-067-5 High Disaster #22	$1.50
☐ 40-423-9 Hijacking Manhattan #4	$1.50	☐ 40-085-3 Divine Death #23	$1.50
☐ 40-424-7 Mardi Gras Massacre #5	$1.50	☐ 40-177-9 Cryogenic Nightmare #24	$1.50
☐ 40-493-X Tokyo Purple #6	$1.50	☐ 40-178-7 Floating Death #25	$1.50
☐ 40-494-8 Baja Bandidos #7	$1.50	☐ 40-179-5 Mexican Brown #26	$1.50
☐ 40-495-6 Northwest Contract #8	$1.50	☐ 40-180-9 Animal Game #27	$1.50
☐ 40-425-5 Dodge City Bombers #9	$1.50	☐ 40-268-6 Skyhigh Betrayers #28	$1.50
☐ 220797-5 Bloody Boston #12	$1.25	☐ 40-269-4 Aryan Onslaught #29	$1.50
☐ 40-426-3 Dixie Death Squad #13	$1.50	☐ 40-270-9 Computer Kill #30	$1.50
☐ 40-427-1 Mankill Sport #14	$1.50	☐ 40-363-1 Oklahoma Firefight #31	$1.50
☐ 220882-5 Quebec Connection #15	$1.25	☐ 40-514-6 Showbiz Wipeout #32	$1.50
☐ 40-851-X Deepsea Shootout #16	$1.50	☐ 40-513-8 Satellite Slaughter #33	$1.50
☐ 40-456-5 Demented Empire #17	$1.50	☐ 40-631-2 Death Ray Terror #34	$1.50
☐ 40-428-X Countdown to Terror #18	$1.50	☐ 40-632-0 Black Massacre #35	$1.75
☐ 40-429-8 Panama Power Play #19	$1.50	☐ 40-673-8 Deadly Silence #36	$1.75
		☐ 40-674-6 Candidate's Blood #37	$1.75

Buy them at your local bookstore or use this handy coupon.

Clip and mail this page with your order

PINNACLE BOOKS, INC.—Reader Service Dept.
271 Madison Ave., New York, NY 10016

Please send me the book(s) I have checked above. I am enclosing $_____ (please add 75¢ to cover postage and handling). Send check or money order only—no cash or C.O.D.'s.

Mr./Mrs./Miss _____

Address _____

City _____ State/Zip _____

Please allow six weeks for delivery. Prices subject to change without notice.